'So, how did the children get on with Meg?'

Nick's mouth kicked up in a grin. 'Brilliant—and thank you. I owe you.'

Ronnie laughed. 'I'll bear it in mind, next time I want anything heavy moved.'

'Always a catch,' he said with a smile.

'Of course. There's no such thing—'

'As a free lunch,' they chorused, and laughed together. Then the laughter died, leaving a lingering smile in their eyes, and Ronnie thought she'd drown in those stunning, smoky-blue depths. Oh, Lord, she thought, he's gorgeous. I could love this man so easily…

Caroline Anderson's nursing career was brought to an abrupt halt by a back injury, but her interest in medical things led her to work first as a medical secretary and then, after completing her teacher training, as a lecturer in Medical Office Practice to trainee medical secretaries. She lives in rural Suffolk with her husband, two daughters and assorted animals.

Recent titles by the same author:

PRACTICALLY PERFECT
AN UNEXPECTED BONUS
SARAH'S GIFT
CAPTIVE HEART
DEFINITELY MAYBE

THE GIRL NEXT DOOR

BY
CAROLINE ANDERSON

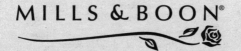

MILLS & BOON®

First published in Great Britain 2000
Harlequin Mills & Boon Limited,
Eton House, 18-24 Paradise Road, Richmond, Surrey TW9 1SR

© Caroline Anderson 2000

ISBN 0 263 82221 4

Set in Times Roman 10½ on 12 pt.
03-0003-50122

Printed and bound in Spain
by Litografia Rosés, S.A., Barcelona

CHAPTER ONE

It was a gloriously sunny day at the end of January, ridiculously hot for the time of year, and Ronnie was cleaning her windows.

She hated cleaning windows, especially with that bright and beautiful sun pouring through the glass and highlighting every streak. She sighed and attacked a particularly stubborn mark again, then paused, her eyes focusing beyond the windows to the car pulling up on the drive next door.

'Next door' was the other half of her house—or the hospital's, to be exact. It had been empty for a couple of weeks, and she had been awaiting the new arrivals with interest and a certain amount of trepidation. Would they be civilised? Noisy? Teenagers with too much bass and too little discipline, like the last lot? Or perhaps a screaming baby to keep her awake all night, just for a change!

Abandoning her thankless task, she settled her hip more comfortably on the window-sill, tucked a stray strand of blonde hair out of the way and watched as the car came to rest and disgorged its occupants in a flurry of shrieks and wails.

A man—possibly late thirties to forty—tall and lean, with darkish close-cropped hair and sunglasses perched on a slightly battered nose, straightened and shut his door, just as the passenger door behind him flew open and a little girl leapt out.

'Quickly, Daddy! Hurry up!' she begged, hopping from foot to foot.

'I'm hurrying—damn, which key?' she heard him mutter as he fumbled with a keyring, and the child hopped and begged and danced and her eyes grew wider.

Ronnie stifled a smile. Unless she missed her guess, somebody needed the loo—urgently!

'Hang on, moppet,' he said encouragingly. 'Ben, this way.'

Young Ben had other ideas. He was out in the quiet little cul-de-sac, kicking his football and ignoring the man.

'Ben. Now!'

He went, with an impressive show of reluctance that brought a smile to Ronnie's lips, and they trooped up the path to the front door and out of sight, leaving the car doors hanging open in the quiet street.

Without leaning out of the open window, Ronnie couldn't see them any more, but she could hear them through the party wall. She heard footsteps drumming up the stairs, a sobbing wail and a deep groan.

Oh, dear. She didn't make it. Had they got any spare clothes with them in the car?

It wasn't her business. Still, at least there were no teenagers or screaming babies.

With a resigned sigh, Ronnie squirted more special non-streak-miracle-window-cleaner-with-vinegar onto the glass and made a few more random stripes in the grime.

Useless.

'You shouldn't do that in the sun,' her neighbour on the other side called up.

Ronnie laughed and hung out of the window, glad of an excuse to stop again. 'I noticed. Too depressing.'

'Makes them streaky.'

'Meg, they *are* streaky. It just makes it show worse.'

Meg shot a glance at the next-door house. 'You've got new neighbours.'

'I saw. Jimmy'll be pleased—someone to kick a ball about with.'

'Mmm.' Meg looked at the house again, then came up closer. 'I wonder where the mother is.'

Ronnie had been wondering the same thing, but rather more quietly. 'Why don't you ask?' she said mildly, tucking another strand of hair behind her ear, and Meg looked horrified.

'Don't be *silly!*' she almost squeaked. 'It wouldn't be polite!'

And this is? Ronnie thought, stifling a laugh.

'Anyway, I've got to go out and fetch Jimmy from school. I'll let you do it.'

She got into her car and drove off in a mass of grinding gears and protesting tyres. Ronnie sighed. Not a natural driver, she thought with a grimace—just as you aren't a natural window cleaner. Oh, well. Not everybody was good at everything.

She gave one particularly bad streak another half-hearted swipe, and gave up. She'd go downstairs, put the kettle on and offer her new neighbours a drink.

Just out of neighbourliness.

Of course.

She might even be able to find a pair of little knickers or some trousers for the youngster next door. She was sure her niece had left something behind last time she'd stayed...

The doorbell chimed—a ghastly tune that Nick hoped he wouldn't have to tolerate for long—and he abandoned his mopping-up operation in the bathroom and ran downstairs. No doubt it was his brother with the van—and clothes, furthermore, so Amy didn't have to run around naked.

'Thank God you're here,' he began distractedly, swinging the door open, and then his eyes dropped, down from the place he'd expected his brother to be, down about a foot or more to a dainty elf with curious, bright green eyes and a smear of dirt on one cheek. She had blonde hair, streaky and curly, scraped back into a pony-tail, and some of it had escaped and was tickling her cheek.

'Hi,' she said, her voice deeper than he'd expected, low and soft and somehow musical. 'I'm Ronnie—I live next door. I've brought you something to eat and drink. I thought you were bound to be thirsty, and I expect the kids are starving. I know what moving's like, and I just bet the kettle will be the last thing you can find—'

She came to an abrupt halt, as if she realised she was running on, and Nick had to fight down the smile that was threatening to engulf his face.

It must have shown in his eyes, though, because she flushed slightly and gave a nervous little laugh. 'Are you going to take it, or are you on a diet?'

He did smile then. The thought of him being on a diet was just a farce. It didn't seem to matter what he ate, the last few years the weight had just fallen off him.

'Hardly,' he murmured, and took the hugely over-laden tray in his left hand, supporting it easily. 'Thank you.' He stuck the other one out in greeting, and she took it, her cool, slim fingers somehow tantalising in his warmer, firm grasp.

'I'm Nick,' he managed inanely, groping for his mind, 'and somewhere about the place are Ben and Amy. Come on in and meet them. We were waiting for my brother—he's bringing our clothes and bits and pieces in his van. And you're right, the kettle isn't here yet.'

She smiled, her eyes crinkling at the corners as if she did it often, and heat shot through him, catching him by surprise. He stood dumbstruck for a second, then, clearing his throat, he turned away and led her into the kitchen, setting the tray down on the rather tired worktop.

'The fruit cake is my mother's, but I won't be offended if you don't like it,' she was saying. 'There's some shortbread and chocolate biscuits as well, which I thought the children might prefer—oh, and by the way, I found these, and I had a feeling your daughter might need to borrow them.'

'Do you read minds?' he asked, bemused, staring as she pulled little clothes out of a carrier bag.

She laughed. 'No, just body language.'

She held out the tracksuit bottoms, and he took them and held them up, eyeing her over the top.

'They either belong to someone else, or you had a crisis with the washing.'

She laughed. 'My niece's. Am I right? Do you need them?'

He gave a wry grin. 'Thank you. I don't know how you knew, but—thank you.'

He took them upstairs, gave them to Amy and told her to put them on and come down. She was still sitting on the loo, sniffing, but the sight of the trousers and thence dignity encouraged her. She wiped her nose on the back of her hand and slid off the seat.

'Wash your hands,' he reminded her, and went back down to his visitor.

'Thanks,' he murmured, and then the door flew open again behind him, crashing against the worktop.

'Dad, the bathroom's gross—oh. Who are you?' Ben asked, grinding to a halt in the doorway and cocking his head on one side. He looked resentful and unhappy, and Nick sighed to himself.

'Ben, I'd like you to meet our new neighbour— Miss…?'

'Matthews—but Ronnie will do.'

'Ronnie? That's a boy's name,' Ben said scornfully, and Nick wanted to curl up—or strangle him.

He opened his mouth to correct the boy, but Ronnie had got there first, laughing softly. 'Odd, isn't it? But it knocks spots off Veronica, which is the alternative.'

Personally Nick thought Veronica was a very pretty name, but he wasn't about to get involved in this argument. Anyway, it dissolved before it really got going, because Ben spotted the chocolate biscuits and had to be restrained from taking a handful.

'There's apple juice or tea…'

'Juice, please,' he mumbled through a mouthful of biscuit. Nick stuck his head round the door and called his little daughter.

She came trailing down the stairs in tears again, her teddy dragging and bumping down the stairs behind her, and he scooped her into his arms and held her close.

'*Now* what's wrong, sweetheart?' he asked a little desperately.

'Ben said I can't have the yellow bedroom, but I *want* the yellow bedroom. I don't *want* the blue bedroom!' she hiccuped, and buried her face in his neck.

'We'll sort it out in a minute,' he promised, feeling helpless for what felt like the millionth time in the last four years. 'Come and meet Ronnie. She lives next door and she's brought us a drink and a biscuit.'

Her head lifted. 'Chocolate biscuits?'

'Uh-huh—or fruit cake. And juice.'

'Orange?'

'No, apple.'

'I want orange—' she began, but Ronnie cut her off.

'Oh, look, you're just in time for the last two chocolate biscuits—and there's some of my special juice for big girls—are you big enough, I wonder, or should I go home and get baby orange?'

Her head was tipped on one side, eyeing Amy assessingly, and Nick felt his daughter straighten in his arms. She slid to the floor.

'Apple,' she said round her thumb.

'Sorry, I didn't hear that?'

'Apple, please,' she said, taking her thumb out, and Nick wondered if women were born with the gift of communicating with children or if men were just particularly slow to learn.

Either.

Both.

She handed him a mug of tea, hot and steaming, with just the right amount of milk, and a plate groaning with a huge slab of cake.

'Wow,' he murmured, and took them, propping himself up against the worktop and sinking his teeth into the cake with enthusiasm. The cheese roll he'd had for lunch seemed a heck of a long time ago, he thought as the flavours burst on his tongue.

'Oh, wow,' he murmured again, his eyes thanking her over the top of the plate.

She smiled contentedly and leaned back against the cupboards, small, neat hands cradling her mug so that steam rose in front of her face, fogging it slightly.

'It's cold in here,' he said, suddenly realising, and turned to the boiler. 'I wonder how it works.'

She put her tea down, flipped dials, clicked switches

and the boiler roared into life. 'It's been on tickover, to protect the pipes. The hospital usually does that. It's the same system as mine.'

'You could be a useful person to know,' he said with a grin, 'between the boiler and the fruit cake.'

She chuckled. 'You'll need to know all sorts of things—dustbin day, where the supermarket is, how to get to the corner shop, where the nearest decent Chinese take-away is, which pizza place will deliver—oh, do you want the milkman to call?'

'Yes!' Nick gave a bemused laugh. 'You wouldn't like to stick it all down on a bit of paper, would you? I'll only forget otherwise.'

'Consider it done.'

She shrugged away from the worktop and headed for the door. 'I'll get back to cleaning my windows. Ben, there's a boy on the other side of me called Jimmy. He'd be about your age. He's always outside playing football. Perhaps you'd like me to introduce you later.'

He nodded without enthusiasm. 'Don't suppose he's much good.'

'Probably not, but he's in the under-ten town squad. I expect they were short of talent.'

Ben's eyes widened with interest, and Nick watched Ronnie hide a smile.

Damn, she was an expert.

'I'll see you later—I'll bring you more tea when your brother gets here. How many of them will there be?'

'Just him.'

She nodded, poorly concealed curiosity in her eyes, but he didn't feel up to talking about Anna just now. Maybe not ever.

'Thanks,' he said gruffly. 'You've been very kind.'

She smiled again, a quick, fleeting smile, and then she was gone, the door closing softly behind her.

'I want the yellow bedroom,' Amy said stubbornly.

'Well, tough, I'm having it, I saw it first.'

'Only because I had to go to the loo!'

'Too bad. I'm the oldest, I get to choose. Isn't that right, Dad?'

Seconds out, round two hundred and ninety-six, he thought, and dredged up a smile.

'Let's go and have a look. Maybe I can paint the blue one—it's only for a little while.'

'Have you *seen* that *guy*?'

Ronnie looked at Kate's dreamy eyes and laughed. 'Which guy is that?'

'The new consultant—Sarazin. You should have seen him in Theatre—poetry in motion, Ronnie, I tell you. We had an emergency—an RTA, had a fight with a tree. His guts were a real mess. I don't know how we didn't lose him. We nearly did twice, but somehow he managed to sort him out. I've never seen anyone find a leak and plug it so quick.'

'Not quick enough. We had a queue of pre-ops sitting, waiting, while he tied knots in your RTA,' Ronnie told her.

'Oh, believe me, he's worth waiting for! What a star! And then, when it was over, he pulled down his mask and grinned, and he was streaked with blood—I swear, he looked like Bruce Willis at the end of *Die Hard*. Bloody, sweaty, sexy—I thought I was going to melt, just looking at him.'

Ronnie laughed again. 'You're a sad case, do you know that? How many times have you fallen for eyes over a mask?'

'Oh, it works without fail,' she agreed cheerfully,

'but it usually falls apart when they take the mask off. The magic just vanishes.'

'But not this time,' Ronnie guessed.

Kate grinned. 'Absolutely not! Wow. I wonder if his wife realises how damn lucky she is?'

Poor Kate. 'Married?' Ronnie said sympathetically.

'Well, he wears a ring. Might not mean anything, though. Lots of them play away. I might get lucky yet.'

Ronnie felt a chill. And some other woman—some innocent woman who foolishly believed she was loved and cherished—would be unlucky, and probably not for the first time. Ronnie ignored the little twinge of pain. It was only hurt pride, she reminded herself. She hadn't really known David Baker, so how could she have loved him? Kate yawned and stretched, and stood up. 'I'll see you round. Let me know what you think of God's gift when you've seen him.'

Ronnie chuckled. 'I will.'

She watched her irrepressible friend go, then checked her watch. Three-thirty. Time she went back to the ward. The delayed post-ops were due to return from Recovery any time soon, and she ought to be there. One day, she promised herself, she'd have time for a proper lunch-break, instead of snatching a slice of toast in the ward kitchen and surviving till her tea-break—if she even got one.

She drained the last of her tea and headed back, still thinking about the new consultant. So he was good, according to Kate. Well, she ought to know, she'd worked with Ross Hamilton for years, and he was excellent—so excellent he'd been head-hunted to lead a team in pioneering bowel surgery. If Kate thought the new man, Sarazin, was good, he *was* good.

She palmed the door out of her way, automatically

scanning the ward for anything that needed her attention, and her eyes skidded to a halt.

Blue theatre pyjamas, white boots, shoulders to die for—and close-cropped, dark-tending-to-blond hair on a head she was sure she recognised.

She went over to him, smile at the ready, and as he turned his eyes widened in surprise.

'Ronnie?' he murmured.

'Hello, Nick. Are you our new superstar?'

He looked confused.

'I've just been listening to a flattering report of your surgical skills,' she told him. 'If your name's Sarazin, that is.'

He coloured slightly. 'Wildly exaggerated, no doubt—and, yes, that's my name. So, what am I supposed to have done?'

'Your RTA. I gather you're very good at finding and plugging leaks, according to Kate.'

'Ah, Kate,' he said, nodding in understanding. 'She's pretty hot herself. Useful member of the team, she knows her stuff. I'm looking forward to working with her. She's an excellent scrub nurse.'

Ronnie felt a sharp and totally irrational stab of disappointment. 'So, your RTA. How is he?'

'Andy Graham? In ITU. He'll live to drive too fast again, I have no doubt. So, what brings you here?'

She laughed softly. 'I work here—it's my ward.'

He blinked, then seemed to notice her uniform and the badge that said, VERONICA MATTHEWS—WARD SISTER.

'Ah. I didn't see you here yesterday.'

'No, I had a day off. I'm sorry I missed you—did you get a guided tour?'

He nodded. 'Thanks—yes. I've left my registrar

closing, and I thought I'd just check up on my post-ops. Do you know where they are?'

'They're not back yet from Recovery,' the staff nurse told them.

Ronnie nodded confirmation. 'They weren't when I went for tea. They were delayed, of course,' she said with a trace of a smile, and he gave a rueful laugh.

'Yes. I'm sorry about that. The RTA was a little time-consuming, more so than I'd thought or I would have warned you.'

'That's OK.' She let the smile widen. 'Want a cuppa while you wait? You can find your way round a coffee-machine, I take it?'

He shook his head. 'Not coffee. It messes up my mind. I try and avoid it when I'm operating. Tea, though?' He looked hopeful, and she gave in. There was little that needed her attention before the post-ops started to come back down, and until they did she might as well make herself useful, getting to know her neighbour and colleague.

'Come on. Tea it is. I'll put the kettle on.'

Nick wondered if it was to be his destiny, having this beautiful young woman making him tea at regular intervals throughout his life. He followed her into the kitchen, marvelling at how she could manage to look slender and sexy and so downright appealing in such a sexless little number as that royal blue dress, then he came to his senses.

What was he thinking about? She was a colleague—and his neighbour, for heaven's sake! He had to live with this relationship for the next however long, and there was no way this sudden, unheralded and unbidden flicker of interest could be allowed to fan itself into a flame.

Never mind the roaring conflagration he could feel threatening his sanity.

Think of Anna, he thought. Remember her. Remember all of it.

The little flame flickered once and died, extinguished under the weight of all those memories.

'White, no sugar, right?'

Ronnie turned, his mug in her hand, and slopped tea over her fingers. Dear God, what had happened to his eyes? Where had that emptiness come from?

She gave a little yelp and put the mug down.

'You've burned yourself—here, let me.'

He took her hand in his, engulfing her wrist and holding it so her fingers were under the cold tap. Her thigh was pressed against his, her shoulder jutting into his side, and suddenly there was nothing in the tiny room but the splashing of the tap and the sizzling awareness that threatened to set fire to her hip and shoulder and hand. She eased away from him, smiling distractedly and turning off the tap.

'It's fine now,' she assured him, and her voice sounded squeaky and unused. She grabbed her tea and propped her hips against the worktop, getting as far away from him as she could in the minuscule ward kitchen.

'So—how did your move go? All settled in?'

'Yes, thanks. I finally managed to stop the children fighting by promising to paint Amy's bedroom yellow.'

Ronnie remembered the damp, wounded eyes of his little girl, and the sulky recalcitrance of the boy, and wondered again about their mother. 'Did your wife arrive safely?' she asked, and then could have kicked herself because that bleak emptiness flashed again in his eyes, just for a second.

'I don't have a wife. She…died.'

So few words. Such a simple statement. So much grief.

Ronnie felt a huge pain in her chest, the ache of loss for those poor motherless children. 'I'm so sorry,' she whispered. She cleared her throat. 'I had no idea. I do apologise.'

He smiled awkwardly. 'I should have told you.'

'When? On Monday, when I brought you the tea? "I'm Nick and, by the way, my wife's dead"?'

The words hung in the air between them.

Ronnie closed her eyes and shook her head. 'Look, I'm sorry. I'm—I don't know what to say.'

'There's not much left to say, Ronnie. It was four years ago. We're pretty used to it. I imagine everyone's bound to be curious.' He looked around the room. 'I don't suppose there's anything to eat in here? I didn't get any breakfast, and we didn't have time for lunch.'

'Toast?' she offered.

'Please. Lots. I'm starving.'

She put four slices in the toaster, drank the tea that tasted like dishwater and left him to it, promising to call him if the patients arrived.

Nick didn't see Ronnie again to speak to. By the time his patients came back down she was busy with an emergency admission, and he was taken round by the staff nurse.

Odd, the sensation of disappointment.

Odd, and a little disconcerting. He couldn't allow himself to be interested. He had to concentrate on the kids, settling them in to school, painting the damn bedroom, finding a house—the list was endless, time-consuming and left no room for a liaison.

Not that he would remember where to start.

He glanced at the clock on the wall over the nursing

station, and frowned. Were the kids all right with the woman he'd arranged would pick them up and take them home? She was the mother of a boy in Ben's class. Would they like her? Would her kids be all right with them? He wished he'd had time to meet her, but the days had run away with him and they'd only managed to move on Monday instead of last weekend, and he'd picked them up himself yesterday.

Oh, Lord, so many new hazards. Please, God, let it all work out, he thought helplessly.

Then the phone rang, and someone looked up at him.

'Mr Sarazin?'

He nodded, a sick feeling in his stomach.

'Phone call—sounds like a child.'

He almost snatched the phone. 'Hello?'

'Dad, it's Ben. Come and get us *now*.'

He sighed inwardly and stabbed his fingers through his too-short hair. 'Ben, I can't.'

'You must. She's awful.'

'Where are you?'

'Mrs Livermore's. She's in the garden—she doesn't know I'm on the phone. Dad, she's horrid,' he hissed, and then played his ace. 'Amy's crying.'

He stabbed his fingers through his hair again, and rolled his eyes. 'Half an hour, Ben. I'll be there in half an hour. Hang on.'

Ronnie could hear the tears and pleading through the wall, but there was nothing she could do. She couldn't just interfere with every moment of their lives.

She had to leave them alone to sort themselves out. It was no good feeling sorry for them, they had to cope alone. They'd been doing it for four years—more than half of Amy's life, for heaven's sake. It was hardly new to them!

She couldn't interfere. She knew from her own experience that it didn't work.

But she could cook…

Humming contentedly under her breath, she got down her recipe books, flicked through them and stabbed her finger at the answer.

'Chocolate fudge brownies. Excellent.'

She beat and whipped and greased and spread, and by the time she'd finished the oven was hot and the tray of brownies went straight in. Now, a main course. Nothing too elaborate, but something kids would eat.

Toad in the hole. Tasty sausages, fluffy Yorkshire pudding, lots of gravy and bright, pretty vegetables— carrots and broccoli, perhaps?

She was just assembling the ingredients when the doorbell rang. Grabbing a tea towel, she scooped hair out of her eyes, scrubbed her hands and opened the door.

'Are you busy?'

She smiled up into Nick's distracted eyes, more than a little delighted to see him—them, she corrected, dropping her eyes and grinning at the children. 'Never too busy to see my friends. Come on in, I'll put the kettle on. I'm just going to cook supper. I don't suppose you'd care to join me? I get awfully sick of eating by myself.'

'We were going to have pizza,' Ben said sulkily, glaring at his father.

'I hate pizza,' Amy whined, obviously carrying on the same argument. 'I want chicken and mushroom pie and chips.'

'Yuck.'

'Kids, stop it.' Nick met Ronnie's eyes over their heads, and she saw a kind of longing in his face which she quite understood. 'We couldn't impose.'

She gave her most disarming grin. 'Yeah, you could. I'm having toad in the hole, but it's silly making it for one—and I've cooked chocolate fudge brownies so we could have them for pudding.'

Even Ben looked interested, despite his best efforts.

'It's cool with me, I suppose,' he said with a huge attempt at nonchalance, and Amy just grinned.

'I love toad in the hole—and chocolate brownies. Can I have lots?'

'Just enough to fill you up and not enough to make you sick,' Ronnie told her. It was obviously the right answer, because they nodded and headed for the sitting room at her suggestion.

A frown flickered in Nick's eyes as the kids disappeared. 'Ronnie, it isn't fair. You set this up,' he said accusingly.

She smiled innocently. 'How? You came to me, remember?'

He pulled a face, and without thinking she went up on tiptoe and kissed his cheek. 'Lighten up, soldier. No one's an island. It's only supper, for goodness' sake!'

He stood frozen for a moment, then a wry smile twisted his lips and he nodded. 'OK. Thanks. What can I do?'

'Peel carrots,' she said promptly, and he groaned.

'I knew there was a catch. They always say there's no such thing as a free lunch!'

Ronnie just smiled, handed him the potato peeler and a bag of carrots and wondered what it was about a perfectly ordinary man that made him so incredibly, irresistibly sexy. The feel of his cheek, roughened with stubble, faintly scented with something masculine and unravelling...

'So, was there a reason for the visit, or did you just need a referee for the pizza v. pie-and-chips argument?'

she asked, squashing out the lumps in the batter and trying not to think of the scent of his skin and the rasp of his end-of-day shadow against her lips.

He groaned. 'I'd almost forgotten. The child-minder I'd arranged for them after school turns out to be related to Godzilla. I don't suppose you know anyone else in the area who could bring them home from school and tolerate them until I get back?'

'Meg,' she said promptly, meeting his anguished eyes. 'My neighbour—Jimmy's mum. She's a registered child-minder. She looks after two little ones during the day for a teacher, and takes them back to Mum when she collects Jimmy. She could manage, I expect. What school are they at?'

'The local primary—Northgate Avenue.'

'Brilliant. So's Jimmy. I'll ask her.'

He shifted uncomfortably. 'I don't suppose you could ask her now? They refuse to go back there—I had a phone call at work from Ben. He'd sneaked into the hall to ring me while the woman was bringing in her washing. Thank God he didn't get caught. I was scared to death of her when I met her this evening. She probably would have skinned him alive.'

'Who recommended her?' Ronnie asked, amazed that he would leave his children with someone he'd never met.

'The school. I would have been here a couple of days earlier and met her and moved in sensibly, but Ben was in the school football team and wouldn't leave without playing in the match on Saturday, then on Sunday Amy was sick—hence the rush.' He cocked his head on one side and grinned appealingly. 'So—would you?'

Lord, what gorgeous eyes...

'Would I...?'

'Ask her? I need to sort something out for tomorrow.'

She threw more flour and another egg into the batter, beat them in and told him to peel more carrots. 'I'll ask them for supper,' she said and, without waiting for the argument, she slid past him, nipped out of the front door and stuck her head round the open door of Meg's house.

'Anybody home?'

'Yeah—the burglars. What do you want?'

She grinned and went in, propping up the kitchen doorway. 'I've got a job for you.'

Meg groaned. 'Another one? What is it this time? Don't tell me—cleaning your damn windows.'

Ronnie laughed. 'No. Actually, it's a real job, with money. Nick's looking for a child-minder after school to bring the kids home and sit on them till he finishes work.'

Meg brightened visibly at the prospect of a job. 'And the holidays?'

Ronnie shrugged. 'Probably. Don't say yes or no—just come for supper.'

'I've just put a shepherd's pie in the oven.'

'How long ago?'

Meg shrugged. 'Two minutes? Less, probably.'

'So sling it in the fridge and have it tomorrow. Go on. It's toad in the hole and chocolate brownies—and I thought it would be good to see how the kids interact before we said anything to them.'

Meg sighed and reached for her oven gloves. 'Anybody ever told you you're a manipulative little pest?'

Ronnie just grinned and headed back over the lawn, picking her way between Jimmy's abandoned bike and the remains of a broken skateboard.

'They're coming,' she told Nick economically.

His shoulders dropped about a foot, and he seemed to unravel before her eyes. She reached into the fridge. 'How about a glass of wine?' she said with a smile.

CHAPTER TWO

'So, how did the children get on with Meg?'

Nick's mouth kicked up in a grin. 'Brilliant. She's a star. They loved her to death, Ben and Jimmy got on like a house on fire and she spoiled Amy to bits. I had to bribe them to come home!'

Ronnie chuckled. 'Successful, then. That's good.'

'Excellent—and thank you. I owe you.'

She laughed. 'I'll bear it in mind, next time I want anything heavy moved.'

'Always a catch,' he said with a smile.

'Of course. There's no such thing—'

'—as a free lunch,' they chorused, and laughed together. Then the laughter died, leaving a lingering smile in their eyes, and Ronnie thought she'd drown in those stunning, smoky blue depths. Oh, Lord, she thought, he's gorgeous. I could love this man so easily...

'So, how are my post-ops?' he asked, his eyes still locked on hers, and she dragged her own eyes away and hauled in the first breath for what felt like several minutes.

'Fine, I believe. Let's go and see.'

She headed down the ward to the first bay, which contained yesterday's patients. 'Well, they're all still alive,' she said softly, scanning the beds, and he chuckled.

'I've started on the right foot, at least.'

'So it seems. How's your RTA?'

'He should be in here in the next few days—they're

short of beds in ITU so they'll kick him out soon, I expect. He's progressing.'

He picked up the notes from the end of the first bed and smiled at the patient. 'Mrs Dobbs. How are you feeling?'

'Oh, marvellous,' the elderly lady said, returning his smile with a twinkle that lit up her lined face. 'I thought I'd feel much worse than this.'

'That's the joy of keyhole surgery,' he told her. 'Just a couple of little snips instead of a great big hole. Much easier to get over.' He bent over his handiwork, nodded and straightened, covering her gently. Ronnie thought how, often, it was the big men who were the most gentle, as if they'd had to learn the hard way how to moderate their strength.

They moved on down the ward, chatting and laughing with the patients as Nick checked his handiwork and the chart at the end of each bed, then they moved on to the pre-ops, the patients who were in for surgery the following day.

One was Mrs Gray, a young woman, only thirty-two, who was in for surgery to remove gallstones.

Nick perched on the edge of the bed and explained to her how he was going to make just three incisions, one for the laparoscope, the camera which enabled them to see what they were doing, and the other two for the instruments which would remove the gall bladder and the cause of all her problems.

'And then you'll be right as rain,' he assured her.

'I hope I will,' she told him drily, 'because I don't know myself at the moment. I've never been this heavy, and I've tried every diet under the sun. I've done the chocolate diet, and the cabbage soup diet, and the banana diet—'

'Have you ever tried just eating normal, healthy food

in smaller quantities, with a lower fat content, and avoiding snacking? There's a lot of evidence building up that it's faddy diets and disrupted eating patterns that cause gallstones. All the fair, fat, fertile and forty nonsense is just coincidence, and women with the problem are getting younger and younger.'

She frowned. 'So you really think it's just my funny diets that have caused it?'

'Possibly. Anyway, I'll ask Sister Matthews to arrange for a dietician to come and have a chat with you, and we'll see you in Theatre tomorrow.'

They finished the ward round, and as they passed the little kitchen Nick looked at Ronnie hopefully. 'Don't suppose the kettle's on, is it? I haven't got time to get down to the canteen, and they only have vile coffee out of a machine down in Outpatients.'

'Poor boy,' Ronnie crooned sympathetically, and ducked as he swiped at her. 'Oh, if you must. We're quiet for once, and I could do with a cuppa.'

She felt him close behind her as they entered the tiny room, and the subtle, tingling awareness of him made the hair stand up on the back of her neck. He was so close, and yet not close enough—

What was she thinking about? She had to work with him! There was no way she could allow her mind to run off on such a track—especially as it was so one-sided. After all, he was still hung up on his wife, and she was just plain, ordinary little Veronica Matthews, the girl next door.

Then she turned round, and his eyes locked· with hers, and the breath jammed in her chest and nearly choked her.

'Um—tea or coffee?' she asked after an endless silence that neither of them seemed able to break.

'Tea,' he murmured, and it sounded like a caress. He

cleared his throat and looked away. 'Um—tea, please,' he repeated, a bit more firmly, as if he was struggling to sound businesslike.

The kettle was half-full and hot—to Ronnie's huge relief. The thought of standing there in that minute room while the kettle boiled from scratch, with him inches away sending out shock waves, was too hideous to consider.

Well, not hideous. Perhaps too tantalising. Too inviting. Too tempting...

Anyway, she'd probably misread the signals. Either that or it was just sexual frustration. After all, when did a widower with two young children and a demanding career find time for a private life?

In the ward kitchen?

She choked down the hysterical laugh and yanked two mugs off the draining-board. She was being ridiculous. He wasn't really interested—and neither was she. Not if she had any sense. What did she have to offer him?

She almost laughed again. Nothing that he'd want. Nothing that would offer what he needed. Unless she'd drastically misread his eyes, all he was after was a sexual aspirin, and she wasn't in the market for that sort of affair.

Any sort.

Hell, she wouldn't know where to start—

'I don't take it that strong,' he said softly, making her jump, and she realised she'd put two tea bags in his mug and was mashing the living daylights out of them.

'Sorry,' she muttered, and started again, because she'd managed to mangle one so badly it had burst.

Fortunately a junior stuck her head round the door and gave her an apologetic grin. 'Vicky says can you come? We've got an emergency coming up for Mr Henderson and he's due here any second.'

'Sure.'

She slid the almost-respectable mug of tea across the worktop to Nick and threw him a distracted smile. 'Sorry, you'll have to drink it by yourself,' she said, and fled.

Nick felt down in a way he hadn't felt down for ages. The kids were finally in bed, and he opened the French door in the sitting room and stepped out into the dreary little garden. It was as cold as charity, but he didn't care. He didn't really notice, except for his feet, but the cold soaked up through his socks and his toes turned to ice.

Still he didn't go inside. It was too damned empty inside, empty and lonely and cold in a way the temperature itself couldn't compete with.

Go and talk to Ronnie.

He shook his head. It was a lousy idea. Most of his lousy ideas just popped into his head like that, but he never heard a voice telling him to get off his butt and go out and have fun. Just crazy things—like this job. He'd been idly flicking through a professional publication, scanning the jobs without interest, and this one had caught his eye.

Near Anna's parents, yet far enough away not to crowd any of them, a consultancy that had sounded exciting, although he hadn't been sure he'd been ready for such a big leap and huge commitment, with the children to consider—still, the advert had tantalised him.

No, he'd thought. Not yet. He'd dropped the magazine, and then this damn fool streak in him had interfered.

Apply for it.

I can't do it, he'd thought, but he had, and now he was here, away from all his old friends, alone. He hated it.

But he didn't need to go and see Ronnie. The way he felt about her, he'd get himself in all kinds of hot water if he went round there now. He liked to think it was Anna's voice he heard, but he knew better. There was no way Anna would send him round into another woman's arms!

Or would she? She'd been most insistent before she'd died that he shouldn't lock himself up like a monk. Maybe it was her, after all?

In which case, why was she never there when he really needed her? When the kids were sick and he didn't know what to do?

No, it was just his damn fool mind playing tricks and tormenting him. He felt tears sting his eyes. The voice wasn't Anna. She was gone, truly gone, for good.

'I miss you,' he murmured. 'Life's just too damned empty.'

Go and see Ronnie, his alter ego prodded. *She'll cheer you up.*

'No!'

He heard her door open on the other side of the fence, and the clatter of her dustbin, and the ache inside him seemed to ease. It was pathetic, he thought disgustedly, how pleased he was to have her near. Then she paused, invisible behind the fence panel. 'Nick?' she said softly.

'Hi.' Did his voice really sound that eager? Dear God.

'I thought you might be there. I can see your door open.' There was silence for a second, then she murmured, 'Are you OK?'

He nodded. 'Yeah, I'm fine. Just a little…'

'Lonely?'

He laughed, a soft, strangled sound without humour. 'Just for a change.'

He heard her settle herself against the fence, just beside him, and he stood on the step and leaned against his doorframe, just inches away from her, wishing he was nearer. 'Fancy a coffee?' she offered. 'I've just made myself one—you could have it over the fence, if you're worried about leaving the children.'

Or you could come round, he almost said, but he stopped himself in time. 'Thanks—that would be great.'

She disappeared, returning in a moment. 'Here.'

He looked up, and her slim, pale hand appeared over the top of the fence, a mug clutched precariously in it. He took it, their fingers brushing, and heat shot through him. He jerked, sloshing boiling coffee down the inside of his sleeve, and he swore under his breath and blew on his wrist.

'You all right?'

'Slopped it,' he told her economically.

'Whoops. Sorry.'

'I'm fine.' He settled down on the step, his feet curled against each other to keep warm, and looked up at the stars. 'It's a beautiful, clear night. I can see all the way up to heaven.'

Was it something in his voice? Or just the words, or perhaps the fact that he was sitting outside, freezing to death, for no good reason. Whatever, Ronnie seemed to tune in to him.

'You must miss her,' she said with unerring accuracy, after a moment's silence.

Nick swallowed, surprised that she'd read him so easily, wondering if he could talk about it. About Anna.

'Yes—yes, I do. I miss having someone to share things with, and it grieves me that she's missing so much of the children.'

'Tell me about her,' Ronnie asked, and he found he could. He told her things he'd never told anyone, things only Anna and he had known about. Maybe it was having the fence between them, almost like being in a confessional, so they could hear but not see, or perhaps it was because she was just the girl next door, or maybe it was something to do with the gentle caring in her voice and the echo of loneliness he heard there.

Whatever, he told her.

'We met when we were eighteen,' he started. 'We went to the same university. She was doing dentistry, I was doing medicine, and a lot of our lectures coincided. We spent more and more time together, and after a few months we became lovers.'

He paused, remembering the first time—the laughter, the wonder, the tears of joy, and then the beautiful voyage of discovery as they learned about each other. Amazingly, he found he could share it with Ronnie— not the intimate details, but the feelings, the love they'd felt grow.

'She was my best friend,' he went on, remembering, too, the times he'd come home and cried, after he'd started his clinical work and come face to face with the reality of death. He told Ronnie about that as well, and about the mistake he'd made which had nearly cost someone her life.

'She kept me sane. I don't know what I would have done without her. We were married at twenty-one, but we didn't think about children until we were twenty six and I was an SHO. She had Ben, and then two years later she had Amy—'

He broke off, remembering how happy they'd been.

Then, just a few short weeks later, it had all fallen apart. He heard the flatness in his voice, the detachment that always came when he talked about the end.

'She'd had mastitis with Ben. Then, after Amy, she felt a lump. Not really tender, but she put it down to mastitis again. By the time she realised it wasn't and said something, it was too late. She had a mastectomy, radiotherapy, chemo—they threw the lot at her, because she was only just thirty, and she went through hell, but it didn't work. She died a year later of secondaries—metastatic carcinoma of the lungs, liver and spine. Ben was four, Amy was two, I was thirty-one—and Anna was dead.'

He stopped, running out of words, feeling again the frustration of knowing that he could do nothing—he, a doctor, trained to save life, had missed the lump, missed the symptoms, missed everything until it had been too late.

'I'm sorry,' Ronnie said, her voice muffled behind the fence.

Nick blinked and stared up at the stars. Was she up there? She deserved to be. He didn't know. He didn't understand death. Even after he'd held Anna's lifeless body in his arms, he still hadn't been able to understand. Now he could hardly remember her, but the gap where she'd been still yawned in his life.

He was in danger of wallowing in self-pity, he thought disgustedly. It was Anna who'd lost everything, not him. He stood up and thrust the mug over the fence.

'Thanks for the coffee, Ronnie. I'll see you tomorrow.'

She took the mug, her fingers touching his again, warm and gentle. He took his hand away and went inside, closing the door softly. Ronnie didn't need him.

Ronnie went into the kitchen at the front of her house, with the hall between her and Nick, and shut the door firmly. She'd been a fool to go out there. She'd seen him from the upstairs window, standing alone in the garden, his shoulders slumped, his head hanging. She'd known it was asking for trouble, but she couldn't walk away from his loneliness any more than she could stop breathing.

Still, to hear him talk about Anna, to hear the love in his voice, and then the stark despair when he told of the end—what was it like to love so much, and to lose that love?

A ragged sob rose in her throat, then another. She turned on the taps, tuned the radio to a rock station and sagged into a chair, rested her head on her arms and howled.

Then she got up, washed her face, blew her nose hard and turned off the noise. Silly. She'd have to get a grip. There was no room for her in his life, and the last thing he'd want was her pity.

She changed into clean jeans and a jumper, grabbed her gym bag and headed for the door. It was late, but the gym didn't close till ten. She'd go and thrash herself around on the equipment for an hour and get him out of her system...

Nick could feel the heat of the lights getting to him. He rubbed his forehead against his shoulder and stretched, easing out the kinks in his back and neck. It was the last op of the morning, and he was tired and ready for lunch.

'Right, I'm going to give you a chance to see what you can do,' he said to Sue Warren, his SHO. 'We're going to make three incisions—here, here and here...'

He indicated. 'And then we'll look and see what we're dealing with.'

He stood back and let the young woman take his place, and over the top of his mask he saw Kate, the scrub nurse, wink slightly in approval.

At least, he hoped it was. He had a horrible feeling he was wrong. He cleared his throat and switched his attention to the operation. 'Right, a little bit farther over—that's it. Now, nice, light, firm strokes with the scalpel—remember we're going for keyholes here, not huge great incisions you can get your arm through.'

'There was a programme on TV about vets,' the anaesthetist mused, checking his instruments and readings with the lazy confidence of long practice. 'There were two vets, one each side of a conscious cow, trying to rearrange her stomach through a hole in each of her flanks. They were shaking hands through the cow's insides while she just stood there and ignored it all.'

'Oh, gross,' Kate said, and shuddered.

'You suggesting we should try it on the patients?' Nick said with a chuckle. 'Now, stand still, Mrs X, we're just going to see if we can find your stomach—'

'How do I do the next one?' the SHO asked, her voice a little tense. Nick forced himself to concentrate on her.

'Same, but different angle—like that. Excellent. Now, this lady's been suffering from intermittent colic. What do you suppose that would indicate?'

'Lots of small gallstones?'

'Yes, most likely. Some people have literally hundreds of tiny, gritty calculi, others have just one huge rock that totally blocks the gall bladder. I suspect this will be somewhere in between.'

Nick worked his shoulder round again. It was aching—no doubt from painting Amy's room last night. Still, at least it was yellow now instead of blue—even if she had had to camp on her brother's floor for the night while it dried.

He looked at the TV monitor, now showing a picture of the inside of their patient. 'Right, you see that dark red mass? That's the liver. Where do you need to go to look for the gall bladder?'

'Um—here?' the SHO suggested, moving the probe carefully towards the right area.

'Good. Let's find out what's inside.'

The operation proceeded without incident, to the SHO's relief, and Nick's prediction that there would be several small stones proved correct.

'We'll put them in a bottle for her—she can have them on the mantelpiece as a trophy,' Nick said with a chuckle. 'Right, would you like to close for me, please?' He watched her finish, then he stepped back, stripped off his gown and gloves and dropped them in the bin on the way through to the changing room.

He took time to shower and clean himself up, even though he was starving, but he had a clinic and they'd run over because his SHO had been naturally cautious. Damn. He probably wouldn't have time for lunch.

He palmed the door out of the way and almost fell over Kate.

'Sorry,' he apologised, catching her elbows to steady her.

'Don't apologise—actually, I was waiting for you, but I wasn't expecting you to be in such a hurry. I've got a favour to ask you.'

He resisted the urge to look at his watch, but his stomach growled loudly. 'Is it quick?'

'We could chat over lunch,' she suggested, and he felt a sinking feeling in his gut.

'No time, really,' he lied guiltily. 'Will it keep till Monday?'

She shook her head, her eyes assessing him. 'It's actually about next weekend—Saturday night. It's the hospital's League of Friends Valentine Ball. My escort can't come. I've got a spare ticket. I wondered if you'd care to come with me.'

He looked into her eyes again and recognised the look for what it was. Oh, hell. 'Um—well, I'm very flattered, Kate, but—ah—the thing is, I—um—I'm already taking someone,' he finished on a flash of inspiration.

Her face fell slightly in the brief millisecond before she slid a mask into place. Damn. He didn't want to hurt or alienate her, but he had very strict rules, and they precluded tangling with workmates.

'Not to worry. No doubt I'll see you there—save me a dance.'

He forced a smile. 'My pleasure. I'll see you on Monday.'

He fled, wondering how on earth he could get himself out of this mess, and then inspiration struck. 'Ronnie,' he said, and almost crumpled with relief.

'Help me.'

Ronnie looked up into Nick's laughing, frantic eyes and felt a bubble of happiness tickle her throat. 'Give me one good reason why I should.'

He closed his eyes and groaned. 'I mean it, Ronnie. I've got myself in a mess.' He looked round them at the crowded ward. 'Is there somewhere we can go?'

She was busy, but not too busy. Besides, her curiosity was piqued. 'The kitchen?'

'This is becoming a habit,' he said with a sexy, endearing grin that made her want to hurl herself at him and hug him. She grabbed the kettle instead.

'Tea?'

'No time. Listen—um.' He scratched his head, clearly at a loss, and Ronnie put the kettle down and waited. 'Ah, it's—uh—how well do you know Kate?'

'The scrub nurse?'

He nodded, his mouth twisting ruefully. Oh, dear.

'Fairly well. We aren't friends, exactly. I shared a flat with her when I first moved up here. Let's just say—we're different. Why?'

He heaved a sigh. 'It's the Valentine Ball next Saturday, apparently. She…' He scrubbed a hand round the back of his neck, looking uncomfortable. 'She told me her escort can't make it, so she's got a spare ticket and would I like to go with her.'

Ronnie shrugged, feeling a wash of something suspiciously like jealousy. 'So go.'

He rolled his eyes. 'Ronnie, she's a barracuda. I can't go with her. Anyway, I panicked. I told her I was already taking someone.'

'Well, that's all right, then.'

'No, Ronnie, it isn't all right. I'm not taking anyone—but I can't lie. I have to work with her every day.'

'So where do I come in?' she asked, wondering what he was getting round to, and rather afraid she already knew.

'Will you come with me?' he asked, confirming her fears. 'Just to rescue me? I have to go now that I've said I am.'

'So you want me to go with you just so you don't lose face?' she asked with a pang of regret.

'No! To hell with losing face. That's the last of my worries. No, it's Kate. Ronnie, I've got to put an end to her flirting. It's driving me nuts. If she thinks there's someone else, she'll leave me alone. It's one reason I still wear my ring—like garlic, to ward off evil spirits and predatory scrub nurses!'

Ronnie laughed in spite of herself. 'That's too subtle for Kate. She thought you were married and it didn't worry her. She was still keen to have a go. I can't think that you taking me to the ball will put her off.'

'But she's a friend—!' he began, and Ronnie laughed.

'And all's fair in love and war. She'd steal you from me without a flicker of emotion. She's only into one thing, and permanence doesn't feature. You'll have to tell her you're not interested.'

He stared at her in amazement. 'And that will work?'

She shrugged. 'Oh, yes. She won't waste energy on you if she knows it's futile. It's no good being subtle with Kate, she doesn't understand it. You have to be blunt.'

'Blunt.'

Ronnie nodded.

'Fine.' He heaved a sigh and scrubbed his hand through his hair, tousling the short strands and making it stick up. 'So, now we've got Kate out of the way, what do you suggest I do with these?' He pulled two bright red, heart-shaped tickets out of his pocket and held them up in front of her face.

She smiled wryly. 'Find someone to go with?'

He lowered the tickets and met her eyes searchingly. 'Do you already have an escort?'

Her heart thumped and pattered. 'I wasn't going.'

'Will you come with me? Since I've bought the tickets.'

'You may as well use them,' she agreed, wondering if her heart would go back to its normal rhythm in the end or if he'd have to resuscitate her. 'I gather it's quite a good do—the food's supposed to be excellent.'

'So you will come?'

She looked back into his eyes, and knew her heart was finished. 'Yes, I'll come,' she said, and wondered if her voice sounded husky and seductive to him, or if it was just her imagination. She hoped so, or he was going to think she was just as bad as Kate!

'You dark horse!'

Ronnie jumped guiltily and looked up at Kate. 'Oh—hi. What do you mean?'

Kate, grinning broadly and utterly unabashed, dropped into the chair opposite in the coffee-lounge, propped her feet on the low table and eyed Ronnie over her knees. 'Sarazin—the ball.'

She felt colour crawl up her throat. 'Oh. That.'

'Yes, that. Come on, don't play the innocent! When did you meet him?'

'Monday.'

'Monday! You didn't tell me you knew him on Wednesday!'

She smiled awkwardly. 'I didn't know I did. He moved in next door—I gave him a cup of tea, and then I had a day off yesterday.'

'And you've grabbed him for the ball before the rest of us got a look-in. Well, I must say, if it was anyone else I'd be irritated, but it's high time you had a fling.'

'It's only a ball…'

'Yeah, and I'm Santa Claus! It's the *Valentine* Ball, stupid! Do you know how romantic and sexy they are? The music is enough to get a eunuch interested—every last damn love song, every smoochy number they can lay their hands on—and you're going to be dancing with Nick Sarazin! Dear God. I could be *so-o-o* jealous!'

Ronnie laughed a little breathlessly. 'Smoochy?' she said, panic fluttering in her chest. Oh, lawks. Smoochy. Sexy. Romantic. She was already like an unravelled ball of string, without sexy music and Nick's warm, hard body to turn her into knots.

Damn. Oh, well, it was only a couple of hours. Even she could survive that.

Maybe…

'Daddy, I want *my* bed. I don't like this bed.'

Nick sighed and paused in the act of reinstating Amy's newly decorated bedroom. 'Sweets, it's only for a little while, till we find a house to buy.'

'Let's go and look,' she said firmly, turning round and running downstairs, her teddy clutched in her arms. He followed slowly, wondering how to deal with this. He didn't know anything about the town, where to look, where the estate agents were—anything.

'Amy, not this weekend, love. There isn't time.'

'There *is*,' she said, her chin jutting just like her mother's.

Go and ask Ronnie about estate agents.

He ignored the voice. He could do without throwing himself at Ronnie. Life was complicated enough since he'd rashly asked her to the ball. 'We have to pick up Ben from Jimmy's in a minute—'

'So get him. He can come.'

Nick sat down on the bottom stair and met Amy's determined little eyes. 'I was going to do all the legwork on my own, getting the details and that sort of thing. It's dreadfully boring.'

'I don't mind. I want a new house.'

He sighed again and stood up. 'OK, we'll go and

see if we can find any agents and get a few details, but I don't want you butting in when I'm talking to them, OK? No comments from the peanut gallery, or we'll come home. All right?'

She nodded. He wasn't fooled, but at least he'd laid down the ground rules. Now to find Ben and convince him.

'I don't *want* to go!'

Ronnie paused in her frantic scrubbing of the once-white resin sink and peered through the steamy window. Ben and Nick were standing on the path by her front lawn, hands on hips, nose to nose almost, Nick with his head ducked to Ben's height, Ben with his chin jutted and looking just like Amy in a strop.

She dropped the cloth, rinsed her hands and dried them, never taking her eyes off the scene for a moment. A slow, amused smile played over her face. Father and son facing off, she thought with a chuckle.

'I want to stay with Jimmy,' Ben was saying. 'I don't want to move to some crummy house in the middle of nowhere. I like it here. I'm not going!'

Move? *Move?* Ronnie felt a sick wave of disappointment wash over her. She didn't want them to move either. In a few short days she'd got very used to them next door—hearing their voices through the paper-thin walls, watching their comings and goings—looking out for Nick when he didn't know she was there.

He slept on the other side of her bedroom wall, the head of his bed against the head of hers. She heard him come to bed at night, and sometimes she heard him get up again during the night.

He didn't sleep well, and Amy sometimes seemed to wake.

Well, sometimes…! In the four nights they'd been

there it had happened twice. That was fifty per cent. A sample of four nights was a little small for solid statistics, but she had the definite feeling that Nick really didn't sleep very well, and the night before last she'd thought she'd heard him cry out in his sleep.

She wrapped her arms around her waist and hugged herself. Just thinking about him made her arms ache emptily. Crazy. She shoved a loose strand of hair out of her eyes, picked up the cloth and scrubbed the sink again with renewed vigour.

So what if they were going to move? Of course they were. Everyone always did, and if she wasn't such a sad, sad person it wouldn't matter a damn.

There was a scream from next door, and she flung the cloth down and ran out the front door. Amy was lying face down on the path, Nick heading for her at a run. He scooped her up into his arms and cradled her on his lap, kneeling awkwardly on the gritty path while Amy screamed and sobbed.

'I fell,' she hiccuped, and Nick crooned to her and smoothed her hair and made Ronnie wish it had been her who'd fallen over and torn her knees to pieces, just to experience that loving embrace.

'Come in and clean her up. I've got a first-aid kit,' she told him, and he nodded and stood up, the crying child cradled easily against his chest. He looked so protective and tender and caring, and Ronnie felt her eyes prickle.

'Stupid,' she muttered, shoving the front door out of the way and trying to sluice the cream cleaner off her hands.

'On second thoughts, you can do it—that stuff might not wash off,' she said almost to herself, and rummaged in the cupboard for a big mixing bowl. She filled it with tepid water from the kettle and found some sterile swabs courtesy of the hospital.

'Here.'

'My hands are dirty,' he said, and looked up at her helplessly, a mute appeal in her eyes.

So she tore open the packet of swabs, tipped them into the bowl of water then snapped on a pair of latex gloves, also from the hospital and bathed the poor, torn, skinny little knees while Amy whimpered and clung to her father.

He watched with an agonised expression as Ronnie carefully cleaned out every last tiny piece of grit as carefully as possible, only stopping when she was sure the skin was clean.

'Right, you'll do, little one. How about the hands?'

She held them out. They were grass-stained and a little pink, but unharmed. They must have hit the lawn on the other side of the path.

'Well, I think they'll do, and a little plaster on the knees should do the trick,' Ronnie said, and opened a box of cartoon plasters she kept for children. 'Mickey Mouse?'

'And Minnie,' she said, looking at the other knee. 'One each.'

She stuck them on upside down so that Amy could see them, and then the child slid off her father's lap and looked up at Ronnie. 'We're going to see the 'state agents,' she told her. 'I want a new house so I can have my bed back.'

'I don't want to go,' Ben said again, standing by the doorway with his arms folded and a mutinous expression on his face.

Nick's sigh was quiet but spoke volumes. 'Ben, nor do I, really, but we do need to find somewhere permanent. It won't take long.'

Ronnie stifled a snort of amusement. House-hunting was the most taxing and time-consuming and tedious thing in the world—so why was she suddenly volunteering to come with them and help them find their way round a strange town?

Didn't she have anything else to do with her precious Saturday morning?

Yeah, clean the sink, a little voice said, and she almost laughed. 'Come on, anything beats doing housework,' she said with a grin, and paused before Ben. 'I know a place in town that sells the best ice creams. I'll treat you.'

CHAPTER THREE

'THAT'S a good area.'

'Good?' Nick asked, interested in Ronnie's criteria.

'Decent local schools, mostly private housing, low crime, pleasant, leafy streets—that sort of thing.'

'Is it near our school?' Ben asked, peering at the agent's photo.

Ronnie shook her head. 'No, it's the other side of town—'

'Then it's no good,' he said firmly, and Nick shrugged.

'Is there a similar area near to where we are now?'

'Oh, yes. It's just that decent houses hardly ever come up. People tend to move in and stay forever because it's so nice.'

Great. Nick shook his head despairingly. 'Shall we give up?'

'We could try one more agent,' Ronnie said encouragingly. 'If anything ever does come up in our part of town, it's usually with them. It's a bit of a hike, but it might be worth it. Shall we give it a whirl?'

He almost said no, and then ten minutes later, as they stood outside the agent she'd mentioned, a house appeared in the window, a lovely old brick house, early Edwardian, with a little turret in one corner and lots of big windows to let in the light. The woman was just putting a photo of it in the window display as they arrived, and Ben looked at it and said, 'I want that one.'

'I want the tower,' Amy said.

'Well, you can't have it, you're a girl. Boys sleep in towers.'

'That's not true! Punzel hung her hair over the side of her tower and the prince climbed up and rescued her!'

'It's *Ra*punzel, thicko,' Ben said scornfully, 'and, anyway, it's only a stupid fairy tale!'

Nick felt like banging their heads together, but he restrained himself. He met Ronnie's eyes. 'Shall I go in and ask about it?'

'Why not? It's in the right area.'

He went in. The house was just three or four streets from where they were living, in the same school catchment area, and by chance was fresh on the market and the agent had a key.

'You could go and look at it,' she told them. 'No one else has seen it yet, and the owner has only just put it on the market. We've rushed a few photos for the press but we haven't got any details prepared at the moment. They won't be ready till Monday. It's a bit tatty here and there—it could do with a little love and attention, but it's got a nice garden. A bit overgrown, but it's west-facing—lovely after work in the summer.'

Nick signed in the key book, picked up the bunch of keys from the desk and then grinned at the others. For the first time in years, he felt a surge of enthusiasm and interest in something other than his children or his job. Maybe this house would be the new start that they needed.

He tossed the keys up in the air and caught them, his grin widening. 'Shall we go?'

It was gorgeous. Tatty, old-fashioned and in need of drastic TLC, but gorgeous. Ronnie watched Nick's face as he scanned the beautifully proportioned rooms, and for the first time she caught a glimpse of the man he really was—the man he could have been if the weight of the last few years hadn't been placed on his shoulders.

His eyes were alight and alive, dazzlingly blue, his mouth slightly parted as if he couldn't quite believe what he was seeing, the odd muttered 'Wow' coming from him as he entered another room or saw another lovely feature.

Ronnie felt a lump in her throat, and another pang of sadness for him that Anna wasn't here to share it with him. What a crying shame.

The children, quite untouched by the emotions of the adults, pelted through the rooms, yelling wildly in the echoing emptiness, their feet drumming on the bare boards. They skidded to a halt in the kitchen doorway, however, and Nick and Ronnie peered over their shoulders.

'Oh, yum,' Ronnie said, and started to laugh. 'Purple and orange, seventies-style. How tasteful.'

Nick chuckled, then eased past the children, something clearly catching his eye. He hunkered down and opened a cupboard door, his fingers running thoughtfully over the painted wood. 'These units are solid— they've been painted this ghastly colour, but I've got a feeling it's an original oak kitchen.'

Ronnie went and looked, and nodded. 'I think you're right. If you stripped it and colourwashed it, instead of having this inch-thick chipped gloss paint, it would be right up to the minute. My goodness, it must be worth a fortune!'

They drifted through the scullery behind, hesitated at the back door and then followed the noise of the children back through the house and up the stairs. They were getting a bit excited, and Nick was clearly unhappy to leave them alone.

'We'll do the garden together in a minute. I just want to keep an eye on them. There are signs of damp in one of the rooms, and the floor might be rotten if the damp's come from the roof. It might get worse as we go up.'

It did, but not drastically. They found Ben and Amy in the 'tower', an octagonal protrusion on one corner, not really a tower at all but more of a bay, with five sides projecting to take maximum advantage of the light.

Each side had a window, and like all the windows they were tall with sliding sashes. Some of the sash cords dangled here and there, and the occasional window wasn't quite shut, hanging at a crazy angle in the frame.

Still, it didn't seem to put Nick off. He went from room to room, marvelling at the size, the proportions, the number of rooms—everything seemed a plus point.

'There's a lot of work,' Ronnie murmured, flicking a peeling strip of wallpaper with her finger.

Nick shrugged. 'I'm glad it's as bad as it is, decor-wise, because I won't feel I have to preserve someone else's taste because it was freshly done—and I know they haven't papered over the cracks either!'

Ronnie laughed. 'Certainly not. What you see is what you get!' She went into the bathroom and stopped dead. 'Nick, look,' she called excitedly, and he arrived on her heels immediately.

'Wow,' he breathed for the hundredth time, but this time it really was a find.

The room was original, almost untouched, the vast bath sticking out into the centre with huge ball-and-claw feet, a great brass pipe for the plug and overflow and huge taps over the end sticking out of the wall. The basin and loo were beautiful, with lovely blue flowers all over the outside and inside of the bowls and down the pedestal and foot, and there was a huge wooden seat around the loo. The tiles had an original dado rail at waist height, and were in almost perfect condition.

'It's like a time warp,' Ronnie sighed.

'It's wonderful,' Nick said, running his finger over the surface of the bath. 'The enamel's a bit dodgy, but I'm sure it can be repaired.' He looked up and met her eyes, and his were bubbling with excitement. 'Ronnie, this place is one in a million. I love it. I want it.'

'It's got five bedrooms on this floor, and there's another floor above,' she pointed out, playing devil's advocate. 'Think of the heating bills.'

He shrugged. 'There's more to life than heating bills. We can be hardy. Very good for us. I could have a study in the tower and an *en suite* bathroom, and the children could share this one, and we'll need a guest room.'

'That takes care of this floor. What about the one above?'

He shrugged and grinned. 'TV room for the kids? Studies, when they get older? Maybe an au pair? That would make sense. Let's go and have a look.'

In fact, the upper floor was closed off by a door, and could quite easily be used as an attic for storage and left empty, if he wanted. Ronnie had to admit that the house was wonderful, but she wasn't sure if Nick had any idea how much it would cost to do up.

'It won't be cheap to get it right,' she warned, remembering her father doing up houses and running out of money in her childhood.

'There's no hurry. The roof, the central heating and rewiring, some plumbing—the rest I can do.' He grinned and ran downstairs again, following the sound of the children's excited voices. 'Ben, Amy, let's go and look at the garden.'

Ronnie followed them slowly down, and stepped out into the glorious sunshine of a lovely day. She eyed the brambles, the huge lilac bushes, the overgrown and unpruned roses—and saw instead a swing hanging from the branch of the old apple tree at the end, and a slide and climbing frame, and wooden garden furniture, and Nick sprawled out, a drink in his hand, smiling at her as she walked towards him.

She was holding a tray, and on it were drinks for the children, and some biscuits, and a bottle of juice for the baby—

This was getting ridiculous! She gulped and turned away, blinking away the mist that seemed determined to cloud her vision. If only it was as easy to clear her mind!

She propped her back against the wall and wrapped her arms around her waist, struggling to get her emotions back under control. He wasn't hers! He belonged to Anna, and it was clear he wasn't ready to let her go.

He invited you to the dance, that little voice said, but she ruthlessly ignored it.

'Only because of Kate,' she muttered.

'What's only because of Kate?' he asked, sneaking up on her.

She jumped guiltily and glared at him. 'Nothing. I was thinking about something totally different,' she said, making absolutely no sense.

He gave her a disbelieving look but said nothing more. What was there to say? He probably thought she was raving mad.

'I want to get back to the agent quickly and sign something, before someone else gets in. I've got cash sitting in the bank. Maybe that will buy me time.'

She shook her head and laughed softly. 'This is Suffolk, Nick, not London. There's no rush.'

'Whatever. Kids, come on. Let's go and buy a house.'

'What about a survey?'

He grinned. 'My brother's a surveyor. He can be here by three this afternoon—if I can catch him.'

He pulled a mobile phone out of his pocket, stabbed in the number and stood, tapping his foot, waiting for an answer.

'Richard? Did you have any plans for today? I've found a house.'

It was all tied up by nine o'clock on Monday. Nick was a few minutes late into work, grinning cheerfully, and told Ronnie that the house had passed its survey with flying colours, if you didn't count the wiring, plumbing and heating, all the windows needing repair and the hole in the roof!

'I've instructed my solicitor, and all we have to do now is sit back and wait for a couple of weeks, and it'll be mine!'

And you'll move, Ronnie thought, suppressing the surge of disappointment. She'd deliberately kept out of the way over the weekend, so as to not expose herself to any more heartache than was necessary, but it was a total waste of time.

She loved him. It was as simple and as complicated as that.

He hugged her, in the way one friend hugged another when something good was happening, and left for his outpatient clinic, totally oblivious of the turmoil of emotion he'd left behind.

She buried herself in her work, dealing with Oliver's operation list, soothing and reassuring and checking complicated equipment and administering drugs and generally running herself ragged, but it didn't make any difference.

Nick appeared at lunchtime, just as she was wondering if she should sneak down to the canteen quickly before he finished his clinic.

'Hi. Fancy a bite?'

'I'm busy,' she began, but Vicky, the staff nurse, came up at that moment and revealed her for the liar she was.

'No, you aren't. We're done for now. I was going to suggest you go early, if you could, because I'd like to meet David at one-thirty.'

Ronnie glanced at her watch, playing for time, but the face was unhelpful. Twelve-thirty, it said, and that gave her half an hour before the next shift came on. 'I can't be long, I have to give report to the new shift—'

'I'll do it,' Vicky said cheerfully.

And that was that. She shrugged feebly, gave a weak smile and trailed after him, cursing Vicky every step of the way.

Except after a few seconds she forgot to bother, because actually it was so good to be in his company that she couldn't remember why she shouldn't be enjoying it.

They settled down at a table in the corner once they'd picked up their meals, and she could see he was still excited about the house. 'I've got so much to do in the next couple of weeks. Still, the children are going to Anna's parents for the weekend, so that should give me some time to sort out a builder and plumber. Don't suppose you've got any idea who I should use?'

'Ask Meg,' she suggested. 'Meg knows everyone. If she can't sort you out, nobody can.' She lifted a forkful of rice and chicken to her lips, and caught Nick's eye.

'What's it like?' he asked.

'Lovely,' she mumbled. 'Have some.'

'My fork's got curry on it.'

So she scooped up some rice and chicken on her fork and held it out to him, then nearly dropped it as his firm, well-sculpted lips closed around the prongs. How could something so simple, so mundane, so *ordinary* as eating suddenly be so erotic?

She swallowed, choked on a grain of rice and nearly coughed herself to death.

'Ronnie?'

'Wrong way,' she wheezed, flapping him away and grabbing for her glass of water. Her eyes were streaming, her voice was up and down all over the place and he was watching her with a very strange look in his eye.

Probably debating sending for the little men in white coats to take her away, she thought, and gulped some more water.

'So, anything interesting in your clinic?' she asked when she could speak.

'Uh-huh. Aortic aneurysm—I'm going to try and graft it laparoscopically, because she's in her late seventies and I don't want to mess her about. She's coming in tomorrow, and I'm going to operate on Wednesday.'

'Have you done it before?' she croaked, still struggling with the grain of rice.

'Yes, a few times. Did Hamilton ever do it like that?'

'Ross? Yes, sometimes. He's coming in on Wednesday. I expect he'll come and annoy you in Theatre.'

Nick rolled his eyes. 'Something to look forward to—the outgoing maestro coming back to see what a carve-up I'm making of his firm! I can hardly wait!'

Ronnie laughed. 'Ross is lovely. He's not like that. You'll see.'

'Hmm,' he mumbled, and shovelled in another fork-ful of curry. 'I'll wait to be proved wrong!'

They talked about the house for a while, and then Ronnie, aching inside with hearing about a home that would never be her home, excused herself and almost ran back to the ward.

Vicky greeted her with a grin and a wave, and disappeared for her lunch with David, the boyfriend of the moment and clearly one that mattered.

Lucky girl, Ronnie thought, and threw herself back into her routine. She was tackling some of the paperwork that dogged her existence when Vicky came back and perched on the desk, her eyes bright.

'I don't suppose you want to do me a favour, do you? Only David's invited me to the ball on Saturday, and I'm on a long day, which means I won't have time to get ready. I wondered if you'd swap Sunday for me. I know it means I'll probably get to bed about three and have to be in for seven, but I'll cope. I just want to look my best.'

Ronnie sat back. Sunday off sounded tempting, and she didn't really need time to get ready. It took ten minutes to get home from the hospital, ten minutes in the shower—she'd be ready by eight-thirty at the latest, and it didn't matter if she didn't look stunning. She was realistic enough to know that, even if the thought did hurt.

'Yeah, sure, I'll do that. I don't need long to get ready.'

Vicky's face was puzzled. 'Oh—are you going out?'

'To the ball,' she said, and then realised that she hadn't told Vicky. The girl clapped her hand over her mouth.

'Oh—Ronnie, you can't swap, then. I'm sorry, I didn't realise.'

'It's fine, Vicky. Really. It's fine. Just make sure you're here, sober and ready to work at seven on Sunday, or it's the last favour you'll get.'

'You're a star!' To her amazement Vicky leaned over, dropped a kiss on her cheek and sailed out of the office on cloud nine, leaving Ronnie to consider the folly of working from seven-thirty in the morning to eight at night, and then going to a ball.

She groaned, just thinking about her feet, and then with a sigh she went back to her paperwork. At least she'd get Sunday to lie in bed—

The phone rang, cutting off her train of thought. It was ITU, asking if she could take Andy Graham, the man Nick had patched up the previous Wednesday on his first day. Good heavens, she thought, only five days ago! Was that all it was?

'Yes, we can take him—just. Anything special I need to do? How is he?'

'Stable but still pretty fragile. He's not critical, but he'll need some pretty intensive nursing. He can't do a lot for himself with his fractures.'

'So why isn't he going to Orthopaedics?'

The ITU sister laughed. 'Are you joking? They're bursting at the seams, and Mr Sarazin seems to think he might have further problems with his liver. He wants to keep a close eye with a view to opening him up again if necessary, so it makes sense if he's with you. The orthopods can't do anything but wait and see.'

Whereas we, Ronnie thought with a dry laugh, have nothing at all to do!

She went out into the ward and warned everyone that Andy Graham was coming down shortly, and they cleared a space for him in the single cubicle room beside the nursing station. He would need specialling and monitoring throughout the night, and it was easier to do it in a small room out of the way of the hubbub of the ward.

She put Vicky with him when he arrived, looking battered and anxious and very young. She saw from his notes that he was only twenty, and wondered how his parents felt about almost losing him. Gutted, probably. She bent over him.

'Hello, Andy, I'm Ronnie, the ward sister. How are you feeling?'

'Sore,' he murmured through closed lips. 'I hurt everywhere.'

'I expect you do. We'll give you a minute to settle down from your journey and then we'll make you more comfortable. You just rest for a bit. This is Vicky—she's going to stay with you.'

'Hi,' Vicky said cheerfully, and perched on the chair beside him with his clipboard. 'I'm just going to do your obs and then you can go to sleep, OK?'

He nodded painfully, and Ronnie left them. Vicky knew what she was doing, and there were still a million and one things to do—like that dratted paperwork. Still, today it was quite appealing. She'd just started a period, and she felt heavy and achy and was quite happy to sit down quietly in the corner and deal with the backlog.

'So, what are you going to wear?'

Ronnie looked at Meg as if she were mad. 'Wear? Well, I don't know. That green thing?'

Meg's lip curled eloquently. 'Ronnie, it was nice six years ago. Times change. You need a new dress. We'll have to go shopping. How does your week look?'

Ronnie laughed. 'Hectic. Why?'

'Because I don't have the boys on Thursday mornings so, if you could wangle a late, we could go then.'

She thought, and shrugged. 'I'm on a late. I don't have to wangle anything.'

'Brilliant. We'll have an early start—in town for nine, round all the right places, make a short list, then go and have coffee, decide and go and buy *the dress*!'

'The dress?' Ronnie said, laughing. 'You make it sound like a—I don't know—a real date.'

Meg smacked herself theatrically in the middle of her forehead. 'Silly me. And there I thought a handsome, eligible man asking you to a Valentine Ball *was* a date. How stupid can I get?'

Ronnie coloured and chased a bubble round the top of her coffee. 'Meg, it's not like that. It's only because Kate chased him—I told you that.'

'So you did. I must have misread the look in his eyes the other day when he dropped you at the door and watched you go in.'

Ronnie's head snapped up. 'What look?'

Her friend smiled victoriously. 'Oh, just a look. Just like a child saying goodbye to a favourite puppy.'

Ronnie threw a biscuit at her, and Meg ducked and grinned. 'Tut-tut. I won't give you biscuits if you're going to waste them. So, are we on for Thursday? Because, my dear, date or not, you *cannot* go out in that green thing *again*!'

Ross Hamilton strolled onto the ward on Wednesday morning, looking bright and chipper and very pleased with himself. 'Morning, Ronnie,' he said in his lovely, soft, Scottish burr, and Ronnie found herself smiling almost before she registered his presence.

'Ross,' she said, taking his hands and squeezing them. 'Good to see you. How are things?'

He nodded. 'Fine. Wonderful. The kids and Lizzi have settled well, the boys like the house, although they won't really be there that often now they're away at college—it's good.'

'And the job?'

'Excellent. I love it—well, so far. I still miss this place, though. How's the new man?'

Ronnie felt warmth climb her cheeks. 'Oh, he seems to have settled in well. Kate rather threw herself at him, but apart from that it's all going fine.'

Ross shook his head. 'I can't understand that. You know, people say that about her, but I never had any trouble. Maybe I just don't have what it takes.'

Ronnie laughed. 'Not much,' she said honestly, and it was his turn to colour.

'I'm serious,' he told her.

'Then you're blind, but Kate's not. If she didn't trouble you, perhaps it's because you never noticed anybody except Lizzi anyway, so why would your scrub nurse register?'

Ross laughed. 'Maybe you're right. So, anyway, how are you getting on with him?'

Ronnie shifted a little. 'Um—fine. He's a very reasonable human being. He seems to be an excellent surgeon—he's doing a keyhole aortic graft today.'

'Is he? What time?'

'About ten. She's all prepped and ready. Why don't you go up and see if you can put him off? I told him to expect you.'

Ross laughed. 'Good idea. I might well do that. It would be good to see the team in action again.'

He glanced at his watch. 'I'd better go—I'll need to change if I'm going to observe, and it might be diplomatic to ask the man's permission!'

Ronnie chuckled. 'I would just walk in and frown disapprovingly and see what he does.'

'Have me thrown out, if he's got any sense! No, Ronnie, I think I'll do it diplomatically.'

'You're so boring,' Ronnie told him with a smile. 'Shall I put the kettle on?'

'I thought you'd never ask!' he said with a chuckle, but then the smile faded from his face and he glanced over Ronnie's shoulder. 'Looks like trouble.'

She turned, just as Vicky came running up. 'It's Mrs Foster—her pressure's going through the floor. I don't know what's happened, but I reckon her aneurysm's probably burst.'

'Oh, Lord—Ross, I know you don't work here any more, but would you? I'll ring Theatre.'

She called, warned them there was a crisis coming up and ran to Mrs Foster's bedside. Ross was doing CPR with Vicky, another nurse was opening a giving set ready to insert it, and Ronnie took over from Ross so he could insert the needle and start giving the patient the fluids he'd ordered.

'Spoken to Theatre?' he snapped.

'Yes—they're just closing. There's another theatre empty—Nick's going to scrub and meet you in there. He wondered if you'd like to assist.'

Ross laughed humourlessly. 'I only came for a coffee. Damned Hippocratic oath. OK, let's get this Haemaccel in fast, while we take her up. I reckon we've got two minutes if we're lucky.'

He slapped a bit of tape onto the tube, grabbed the bag of Haemaccel and crushed it ruthlessly in his fist. They kicked the brakes off the bed, pushed the curtains aside and ran for the door.

'Vicky, you stay, I'll take over,' Ronnie said, and they left her at the doorway, heading down the corridor through the stream of pedestrian traffic with yelled warnings to everyone to clear the way, and Ross joking that they needed a flashing light on the end of the bed.

The theatre lift was there, waiting for them with the ODA standing by to help, and without delay Mrs Foster was wheeled into the anaesthetic room. The theatre team took over, leaving Ronnie with a massive surge of adrenaline and nothing to do.

Ross shot off to change, and she caught a glimpse of Nick in fresh theatre pyjamas, diving into a clean gown and heading towards the patient. 'Right, let's get her opened up and see what she's done. Where's that cross-matched blood? It should be here by now.'

'It's on its way—there's two units of O-neg. here.'

'Well, get them in her—what are we waiting for? Let's go.'

The door slapped shut behind them, and quiet descended over the anteroom.

Ronnie turned and smiled at Ross, now changed and scrubbing rapidly. 'Have fun,' she said with a slight smile, and he grinned and winked.

'Put the coffee-pot on. We'll be down shortly to let you know how it went.'

'Consider it done,' she said with another tired smile, and then she turned and went back down to the ward, wondering how they were doing and if either Nick or Ross were clever enough to snatch Mrs Foster back from the jaws of death.

There were always those times when being clever just wasn't enough, and it looked as if this might be one of them.

'You win some, you lose some,' she murmured to herself, and bumped into Vicky.

'Earth calling Ronnie, come in, please,' Vicky said with a smile.

Ronnie sighed and pushed a stray strand of hair out of her eyes, dredging up an answering smile. 'Sorry. I was wondering about her chances.'

Vicky shrugged. 'Pretty grim, I suspect. I've made you a cup of tea. You look as if you could do with one.'

Ronnie did smile then, a genuine smile that reached her eyes. 'You're a love. I can almost forgive you for Saturday!'

'Ah, but you get Sunday off,' Vicky reminded her, and she thought how lovely it would be to wake up on Sunday morning at some ridiculously decadent hour, and be able to enjoy the luxury of not having to get up.

'So I do,' she said with a laugh, 'and you'll be here at seven. Are you sure about this?'

Vicky nodded. 'Absolutely. I need that time to get ready. I'm going to knock his socks off.'

Ronnie didn't think it would be that hard. She'd seen the way David had been looking at Vicky in the last few days, and she had a feeling he was going to propose to her on Saturday night—in which case it seemed unfair that she would have to do Sunday instead of spending it with him.

She spoke without giving herself time to think. 'Look, I don't suppose we'll stay all that late at the ball, so why don't I do Sunday for you and you'll just owe me a massive favour?' she suggested, and the glow in Vicky's eyes more than compensated for the sinking feeling that she'd just thrown away a lovely lie-in!

Oh, well, so she was a regular little angel. How comforting. She'd have to remember that at six-thirty on Sunday morning when she was dragging herself blearily out of bed!

She drank her tea while she scanned the paperwork of the day, checked the list of pre- and post-ops and new admissions, and waited for Ross to come back down and tell her how Mrs Foster had got on.

She could hardly believe her eyes when Ross appeared with Nick, both laughing, and she knew it was all right. Even so, she had to ask.

Nick shrugged and pulled a 'how could you doubt me?' face, and Ross laughed.

'She's gone to ITU. It must have been seeping gently for some while,' Nick told her, and scrubbed his hand round the back of his neck. 'Any chance of a cup of tea?'

Ross looked at him. 'Tea?' he said in disgust, and Ronnie chuckled.

'Yes, tea. Unlike you, he doesn't believe in poisoning himself when he's under pressure. I could make you instant.'

Ross pulled a face and sighed. 'Tea it is, then—good and strong.'

'I've got chocolate biscuits, as you've been such clever boys,' she told them to compensate, and they seemed quite contented. They ate almost all the packet, in the few moments they were there, and then they left again, deep in conversation.

'They seem to be getting on well,' Vicky said, watching them walk up the ward together.

'Mmm. Similar, in a different sort of way. I think they'd make a good team. It's a shame they'll never work together.'

'Well, barring the occasional well-timed crisis,' Vicky said drily. 'It's a good job he was here to help. I don't suppose it was easy once they'd got her opened up.'

'I gather not,' Ronnie said, thinking back through

the snippets of conversation over the tea and biscuits.
'I don't think they had a lot of time to spare either.'

'Brilliant. Just brilliant, the pair of them,' Vicky said
with a self-satisfied smile. 'Aren't we lucky they aren't
stuffy and pompous?'

Ronnie chuckled. She'd worked with some stuffy
and pompous surgeons in her time, and she couldn't
have agreed more. 'Aren't we just?' she said softly.
'Aren't we just?'

'No, I don't like it, it's a rag on you. Try this.'

Ronnie looked at the scrap of cloth dangling from
Meg's hand and rolled her eyes. 'You think *this* is a
rag, and you want me to try *that* one?'

'Just humour me,' Meg said, shoving it at her. 'Go.
Try it.'

She went, and realised instantly that she couldn't
wear a bra with it. Nevertheless, she tried it, and came
out, peering doubtfully over her shoulder at the low-
cut and revealing back, the slit up the side of the thigh
and the sinuous fit of the bias-cut silk.

'It's outrageous,' she said, laughing, and then noticed Meg's jaw hanging.

'My God,' her friend said slowly. 'I always thought
that green thing didn't do you justice. Now I know.
Buy it.'

Ronnie's eyes widened. 'Buy it? But we were going
to short-list over coffee—'

'No need. Buy it. We can have more time over coffee—maybe wallow in a really sinful cake, oozing with
cream...'

Ronnie snorted. 'You must be kidding. If I just lick
your plate I won't fit into this dress!'

'Yeah, you will. It's bias-cut—it expands.'

'And lovingly outlines every little bulge.'

Meg rolled her eyes. 'You have no bulges. You're talking nonsense. Just pay the woman and let's go. I'm starving.'

She changed, paid and went, feeling hustled and a little uneasy, but with a bubble of happiness tickling her throat. She hadn't had a new dress—not one like that, at least—for years.

Too many years.

She tried not to think about how many years, or that buying it for Saturday and Nick was probably a waste of time.

'Stop it,' Meg said. 'You're wrong about him. If he can resist you in that, he's too cold-blooded to be worth bothering with. Incidentally, you know you can't wear knickers under it, I suppose?'

Ronnie slammed on the brakes and came to a halt in the middle of the pavement. 'What?' she squeaked.

'VPL—visible panty line. You'll have to wear those tights with a built-in gusset—or nothing, of course,' Meg said with a wicked wink. 'That should get him going.'

Ronnie laughed a little awkwardly. 'But what if it's just lust?'

'What of it?' Meg said with a shrug, heading into the little coffee-shop. 'Even lust would make a refreshing change, after all this time! Get real, Ronnie. You need a life. This is just a step in the right direction. Now, coffee and walnut, or double chocolate heaven?'

She stared at them, gave up trying to choose the low-calorie option and plumped for the double chocolate heaven with cappuccino. So what if she had a bulge by Saturday? It might be the only thing that kept her out of trouble!

CHAPTER FOUR

SATURDAY was a nightmare. There was only one thing Ronnie hated more than a 'long day'—seven-thirty in the morning to eight at night—and that was an overly busy one.

It should have been quiet, but Mrs Foster, with her extensive surgery following her ruptured aneurysm, came back from ITU because they were short of beds, and Andy Graham was still feeling pretty rough. One of Oliver's patients admitted overnight was still in need of close supervision, and there was another one in Theatre who would be coming down soon.

Thus, apart from the usual chaos of patients going home after minor surgery on Friday, patients going home after slightly more major surgery on Wednesday and the normal busy ward routine, she had to organise two nurses to special her more critical two—and she was two nurses short! Great!

Mrs Foster was particularly unhappy because, if all had gone well, she might have been going home either that day or the following Monday, and as it was she would be in hospital now for several more days. 'Still,' she said tiredly, 'I suppose it might have been worse.'

'It might indeed,' Ronnie agreed, checking her obs and wondering why it was that with the ward at full stretch she was two staff down. On quiet days they were all there without fail—not that they got many quiet days. Maybe she'd ring Vicky and ask her to come in till three. That would help.

She settled Mrs Foster, asked a health care assistant

to keep an eye on Oliver's post-op for a moment, and rang Vicky's number.

There was no reply. 'Typical,' she sighed, and was about to hang up when Vicky answered, a little breathlessly.

'Do you remember that favour?' Ronnie began, and Vicky groaned.

'What, now?' she said, guessing.

'I'm two qualified staff down, and the hospital's at full stretch. Just till three, Vicky—please?'

'Three? Promise?'

Ronnie looked round the ward and rolled her eyes. 'Promise.'

'OK.'

'You're a star.' She hung up and went back to the patient, and let the HCA carry on with her work. Vicky would be there soon, and she could go and deal with the discharges.

In the good old days, of course, she wouldn't have had to worry about discharges on a Saturday. They simply would have stayed in another three days. Now, patients went home as soon as possible, to cut waiting lists and keep staffing costs down. If that meant chaos on the weekend, well, they could deal with it, and there was a part of Ronnie that thought people recovered much quicker at home anyway.

Peace and quiet was in very short supply in a modern hospital, and everybody needed peace and quiet to heal.

She'd needed it after David Baker and his emotional blackmail and infidelity, and it had been impossible to find anywhere to go. In the end she'd had three weeks off and gone to a Scottish croft and cried her eyes out. Then she'd come back steaming mad, thrown anything of his she'd found out of the window of her flat, handed in her notice and moved here.

It was the best thing she'd ever done, but it had been six years now, and maybe it was time her personal peace and quiet came to an end.

It was a bit of a scary thought. She wondered if she had the guts to wear the dress—especially with no knickers—and almost panicked. She'd considered buying a thong so that she didn't get Meg's VPL, and decided it was better to wear tights with a nice opaque top, which were infinitely more comfortable and felt safer.

Slightly.

Oh, Lord.

She was so out of touch with clubs and pubs and parties and balls. It was ages since she'd been to anything other than the most informal get-together, and then she'd slipped off as soon as it had been decent.

What if she was bored? she thought, and then imagined being bored while she was in the same room as Nick, never mind in his arms, and almost laughed aloud.

OK, so she wouldn't be bored. Would he?

Ronnie's heart started to hammer. Oh, dear heaven, what if she sent him to sleep? David Baker had never found her riveting—

'Why are you scowling?'

Her head flew up and she met Nick's eyes, crinkled at the corners with a smile that made her heart thump even faster. 'Just thinking about tonight,' she said without thinking at all, and then hurried to explain as a frown creased his brow. 'I mean, I was considering what to wear with my dress,' she elaborated, in case he thought she was scowling about going out with him. 'You know—accessories.'

'Shoes, jewellery, tights—underwear?' he suggested softly, his eyes laughing again, and she thought better

than to explain to him that there would *be* no underwear! He need never know, thank God. She looked
quickly away.

'Shoes,' she lied. 'I was wondering which shoes. I
want to be able to walk tomorrow—I'm on duty again
at seven.'

Nick frowned again. 'Tomorrow? But I thought you
had tomorrow off?'

'I did,' she explained ruefully, 'but I think Vicky's
David is going to pop the question, and I thought they
might like Sunday together to celebrate.'

'So you offered to do Sunday for her.'

'For my sins. Still, Vicky's coming in now to give
me a hand just until three, so I'm getting my own back
a bit.'

He nodded. 'How is Mrs Foster?' he asked.

'All right. Tired and fed up, and a bit tender. I think
her bowel has started to work again, I could hear
sounds a little while ago.'

He nodded again. 'Try her with a little water later.
Just ten mils at a time at first, I think. She's been quite
poorly after all that pulling about.'

'OK.' She jotted it down on a scrap of paper in her
pocket and stood up, moving out of the room so they
didn't disturb the patient. 'So what brings you in on a
Saturday?'

'Can't stay away. It must be you.' He grinned. 'Actually I wanted to check on Mrs Foster and make sure
my discharges were all OK to go home, which they
seem to be. I couldn't find you.'

'I've been in here.'

'So I realise.' He pulled something out of his pocket
and showed it to her. 'Just been choosing carpet for
the house. I thought of having this cream in the drawing room. What do you think?'

Ronnie winced and took the little sample of pale, soft carpet, and imagined it with football boots and chocolate ground into it. 'Cream? Do you think that's wise?'

He laughed. 'Probably not, but we've got a snug which we'll use most of the time, and children and animals will be banned from the drawing room unless they're inspected and shoeless.'

She shook her head, laughing. 'You're nuts. What about the rest?'

'Green—soft jadey grey-green. I couldn't get a sample of that, he wouldn't cut it off the book, but it's a lovely colour and it'll go with the suite for the snug. We had something similar in the other house and it was brilliant for not showing dirt.'

Ronnie chuckled. 'Sounds like a good idea.'

He glanced at his watch and pulled a face. 'I'm meeting the electrician at the house in half an hour. What time will you be ready to go tonight?'

'About eight-thirty,' she told him, and hoped there weren't any complications.

'Sure?' he asked doubtfully, clearly not believing her.

'I don't take long to get dressed.' Especially when I'm wearing *so-o-o* little! she added to herself, and felt another flutter of panic.

'Just so long as we don't miss our dinner.'

She smiled and patted his cheek. 'You won't miss your dinner, don't worry. I'll be quick.' She dropped her hand, turned round and surprised by a look of fascinated curiosity on Vicky's face.

'Ah, Vicky, I'm glad you're here,' she said quickly to cover her confusion. 'Could you special Mrs Foster for me, please?'

And with that she waggled her fingers at Nick and

the fascinated Vicky, and disappeared down the ward to see to her other patients.

'Oh, dear God, I can't wear it!' Ronnie wailed, studying her reflection with something akin to shock. 'I look ridiculous! I'm going to wear the green—'

'Don't be absurd, you look gorgeous. Don't you *dare* change. Here, let me do something with your hair. It needs to be up.'

'It's always up, I thought it needed to be down...'

'It's always up *tidily*. It needs to be up *untidily*—you know, bits sticking out and little tendrils.'

'You make it sound like a badly trained honeysuckle,' she said with a laugh, and let Meg push her into a chair and fiddle with the still slightly damp mess on her head.

'Right, that should do. Got any pins?'

She reached for a box. 'Is the Pope Catholic? I wear my hair up every day—of course I've got pins—ouch!'

'Sorry.' Meg tweaked and teased and combed, and then stood back. 'Tiara. No peeking,' she said firmly, and vanished. Ronnie, overruled and defeated, sat there and waited for her to come back. She was only gone for what seemed like a few seconds, then she was back, a little crescent of sparkles clutched victoriously in her hand. With a laugh of triumph she plonked it on Ronnie's head and stood back.

'Excellent. Have a look.'

Ronnie hardly dared, but time was running out. She stood up, turned round—and gasped. 'Good Lord,' she breathed, and bent forward, studying the intricate tweaks and loops Meg had ingeniously worked into her hair.

'I used to be a hairdresser in a previous incarnation,' Meg explained.

'You dark horse,' Ronnie murmured, examining the overall effect. 'Wow. You're a love. Thanks.' She kissed Meg's cheek, grabbed her coat and bag and headed for the door.

'Drop the catch behind you—I have to fly!' she said, and she ran downstairs, putting her shoes on as she went, hopping to the door. She tugged it open and found Nick standing there, stunning in a dress suit with a long white scarf and black coat. He looked good enough to eat, and Ronnie's mouth all but watered.

Nick seemed to be having trouble as well. He did a mild double take, collected up his jaw and grinned. 'You look—gorgeous, Ronnie,' he said gruffly, and, taking her elbow, he shot a grin at Meg over her shoulder and seated her in his car as if she were a princess.

Ronnie found her heart somewhere up round her tonsils, drumming away like a mad thing. She gulped to push it back down, and took slow, steadying breaths to calm herself.

Suddenly it began to feel very much like a real date!

Nick couldn't believe it. All these years he'd shut himself away, not looking for anything except peace, and now suddenly he felt as if the safe, secure, familiar ground had been snatched out from under his feet, tumbling him into a strange place filled with forgotten emotions and wild longings—and Ronnie.

She looked stunning. That dress—it fell softly from a demure, high neckline, draping across her bust very discreetly, and from the front it looked entirely proper. Then he'd caught sight of the back, dipping away towards the hollow of her waist, and he'd nearly had a stroke!

He'd only invited her to protect himself from Kate—and now it seemed she was proving to be much more dangerous than Kate could ever be. Ronnie, his nice, safe, cheerful little next-door neighbour, full of useful advice about the milkman and the boiler, and Sister Matthews, crisp, efficient, kindly—they were gone, and in their place was another woman he'd never seen before.

Warm, soft, a little shy, with feminine curves and an elegance he'd never even guessed at—she was stunning. He dragged in another breath—just now he seemed to be having to tell himself to breathe all the time—and tried not to ogle.

They were in conversation with Oliver Henderson and his wife, and a group of others he'd not met, and Ronnie was standing next to him, so close that the delicate fragrance surrounding her teased his senses still further. Somebody pushed past him and he stepped forward, bringing his body hard up against hers.

Heat shot through him, and he was only too relieved when the person moved out of the way and he could step back.

'Sorry,' he murmured, and she smiled up at him. His gut clenched, and he had a feeling he probably looked a little ridiculous, but he couldn't drag his eyes off her.

His life was saved by the announcement that dinner was to be served, and they were able to move through to the buffet and break the tension that was threatening to kill him.

Maybe Meg was right, Ronnie thought, catching Nick's eye for the umpteenth time and surprising what could only be called a 'look'. Dinner seemed to drag for ages, and all she wanted was for it to be over and the dancing to start.

And then it *was* over, and he stood up and held out

his hand. 'May I have the honour?' he said, and his voice sounded a little rusty.

'Thank you.' She tried to smile, but her face felt frozen with anticipation.

Lord, woman, it's just a dance! she told herself. He's not going to make love to you on the floor! Her heart hiccuped at the thought, and she had to stop herself from hyperventilating.

The first few dances were quite lively, and they warmed her up and relaxed her. She started to smile again, and Nick returned her smile and winked. He looked a little relieved, as if he'd been worried about her, and she couldn't work out why—unless she'd looked as if she hadn't been enjoying herself!

She let her smile widen, and then suddenly the music slowed, changing to a soft, romantic number, and her smile slipped.

Their eyes locked, he held out his arms and she stepped into them and felt as if she'd come home.

Even though he was so much taller than she was, her head still seemed to fit just right into the curve of his shoulder. His hand lay against her back, his finger-tips cool against her skin and yet burning her with awareness. She settled against him, and felt the solid brush of his thighs against her legs.

He held one of her hands in his, clasped between them so that the back of his hand was lying against her breasts through the soft silk of her dress. Her left hand lay on his shoulder, feeling the powerful ripple of mus-cle underneath through the fine wool of his jacket. She wanted to take the jacket off, to explore him, to get to know every hill and valley, every plane, every angle of his body.

She wanted him, and the wanting made heat pool in her and turned her legs to jelly. Someone bumped into them and pushed her harder against him, and she felt a sudden shock of awareness.

He wanted her, too! Dear God. Shivers ran over her skin, and she lifted her head and looked up into his eyes. They looked dazed, a little puzzled, and with a groan he cupped her head in his hand and tucked it back under his chin.

His arms slid round her, his hands hot against her spine, and she slipped her arms under his jacket and circled his waist. He was hard and lean and fit, firm columns of muscle bracketing his spine, and she could feel the heat coming off him in waves.

They swayed gently to the music, oblivious to their surroundings, and all Ronnie could feel was the hard warmth of his body and the beat of his heart slamming against her ear.

They danced like that for hours, through the fast numbers as well as the slow, only pausing every now and again for another drink of mineral water to cool them down.

It didn't really work. It would have taken bucketfuls to make a difference, Ronnie thought. And Kate had been right—it was *the* most romantic evening. She saw Vicky and David glide by on cloud nine, and caught the faint sparkle of a ring on Vicky's finger.

So he had proposed, she thought, as Nick drew her back into his arms, and then she forgot about Vicky and David—forgot about everyone and everything except Nick and how good it felt to be in his arms. As the emcee wound up at the end of the night, they stepped reluctantly apart. 'We'd better go before the car turns into a pumpkin,' he said gruffly, and she somehow managed to remember how to smile.

They retrieved their coats from the cloakroom, and went out into the bright, frosty night.

'Oh, it's cold!' Ronnie said, shivering involuntarily, and his arm came around her and held her against the shelter of his side.

'The car's not far,' he murmured, and then they were rounding the corner and he was putting her in the seat and sliding behind the wheel.

And now what? Ronnie thought on the drive home. She felt suddenly terrified that he would kiss her good-night politely at the door—and terrified that he wouldn't. Oh, help.

He pulled up outside, cut the engine and looked across at her. 'Come in for a while,' he said, and she realised she'd been much more terrified that he *wouldn't* ask her in!

'Just for a minute,' she agreed, and wondered if she'd be able to walk with her heart in her throat and her knees on strike. Apparently she could, because she found herself inside his house, kicking off her shoes and heading for the kettle without giving herself time to think.

'Ronnie?'

'Tea or coffee?'

'Veronica?'

That stopped her in her tracks. She put his kettle down and turned slowly round, and was stunned by the raw desire she saw in his eyes. 'Come here,' he commanded softly, holding out his arms, and she went into them as if he'd reeled her in.

'You are utterly gorgeous,' he murmured, and then her chin was cupped in his strong, clever hands and his lips settled on hers like a sigh.

It wasn't enough. She opened her mouth to him, desperate to be closer, to taste him, to know all of him, and he groaned deep in his throat and engulfed her mouth with his.

She made a little noise, a trembling sigh of surrender, and she felt his hand glide up her thigh and curl around the swell of her hip, drawing her nearer.

'Veronica,' he whispered unsteadily, and his mouth found hers again, wild and demanding. It found an answer in a ravaging need she'd never known she possessed.

She needed to touch him, needed to hold him, to be one with him, without any barriers between them. He must have read her mind, then, because somehow they were together, so she couldn't tell where she ended and he began, and as she gave herself to him she felt an incredible rightness, a wholeness, as if for the first time in her life she was truly complete...

Ronnie ran her hand gently down Nick's spine, feeling the damp satin of his skin against her palm, loving it. Loving him.

Her lover.

Emotion welled in her, and she opened her tear-filled eyes and found him staring down at her, his face stunned.

'Dear God,' he whispered raggedly, and then wrapped her in his arms and cradled her against his shoulder. 'Ronnie, I'm sorry, I never meant this to happen. I just wanted—I didn't want the evening to end. I never dreamt—' He broke off, dropping his head against her shoulder, and another shudder ran through him. 'It just caught me by surprise. You caught me by surprise.' He sounded shell-shocked. She could understand that. She felt pretty shell-shocked herself.

She threaded her fingers through his hair and kissed him. 'Nick, it's OK. It caught me by surprise, too, but that doesn't mean I mind.'

He raised his head and looked around. 'We didn't

even make it upstairs,' he groaned, and started to laugh softly.

'No, and this floor isn't exactly yielding,' she said with a shy smile.

'Oh, Ronnie, I'm sorry.'

He rolled away from her, kicked away his trousers and scooped her up into his arms. 'Let's do this properly,' he said with a lazy smile, and carried her up the stairs to his bedroom. Then he lowered her feet to the floor, sliding her down his body so that she felt every inch of it, and then he stood back and stripped off the rest of his clothes.

He was beautiful. Firm, lean, his body well muscled and yet not heavy, Ronnie thought she hadn't seen anything so beautiful in her life. She reached out to lay a hand on his chest, curious to test the texture of the light scatter of hair, but he stepped back out of reach.

'Undress for me,' he said gruffly, and with a racing heart she turned around, pulled the hem up over her head and let the dress fall to the floor, leaving her naked. Meg's creation was starting to fall down, so she pulled out the pins and shook her head, sending her hair tumbling over her shoulders.

She heard his breath catch and a second of shyness gripped her, then she told herself not to be silly. This was Nick. She loved him. Of course he could see her.

And then she turned, and caught a look of shock on his face.

'Nick?' she murmured.

'Oh, God,' he said rawly. 'I didn't think…' He stared at her body, his eyes anguished, and then he covered his face with his hands and turned away. 'Oh, my God. I'm sorry, Ronnie. Give me a minute.'

And then she remembered Anna—Anna, whom he'd

loved more that life itself, who'd died of breast cancer after a mastectomy.

Tears filled her eyes, and she picked up the dressing-gown lying on the end of his bed and slipped it on. It drowned her, but it didn't matter. Perhaps it was even better that way. She turned up the cuffs, tugged the belt tighter and went over to him.

'Nick? I'm sorry,' she said gently, struggling to control the sadness that was threatening to overwhelm her.

He dropped his hands and stared at her. 'Sorry? Why ever are you sorry? You've done nothing wrong—nothing.'

'It's Anna, isn't it?'

He shuddered and looked away. 'I haven't made love to anyone since her. We didn't get round to undressing downstairs, so it didn't hit me. It was only now, seeing you like that—so beautiful—so whole—'

He broke off and tears filled his eyes. He ignored them and went on, anger in his voice. 'I should have noticed, Ronnie. I'm a doctor, for heaven's sake! I should have noticed there was something wrong with her. God knows, I touched her enough. You'd think I would have felt something…'

He closed his eyes and the tears hovered on his lashes for a moment, then slid heavily down his cheeks. 'I'm sorry,' he whispered. 'I didn't realise it would get me like this.'

Ronnie's heart overflowed with sadness, not just for Nick but for herself. She needed him so much, now more than ever, and yet it suddenly seemed as if there was no place for her here with him. 'Do you want me to go?' she asked in a strained voice.

'No!' He reached out for her, drawing her into his arms. 'No, of course I don't want you to go. It was just the shock. It just hit me—the guilt, again.'

'You've got nothing to feel guilty about, Nick,' she told him, aching to reassure him, uncertain that she could get through this conversation without falling apart. 'It wasn't your fault. It was just a cruel twist of fate. Most breast cancers in young women are too aggressive to treat except in the very early stages. You know that.'

He nodded wearily. 'I know. I just—I know it's irrational, but I thought if I'd checked her, I would have made her do something sooner.'

'And it would probably still have been too late.'

'Yes.' He lifted his head and tipped her chin up to face him. 'Let's go to bed.'

'You want to?'

His hand cupped her cheek, his face so gentle, so loving, so vulnerable. 'Oh, yes. More than ever. I need you, Ronnie.'

She nodded, understanding, knowing he was using her and yet unable to walk away from his need. 'Yes,' she whispered, and he tugged the belt free and slipped the dressing gown off over her shoulders. It puddled on the floor at her feet, and he looked down at her, at the soft fullness of her breasts, pink-tipped and puckering with the cool air, and sucked in his breath.

'Touch me,' she said, wondering if he could or if Anna would get in the way, and his hands came up, trembling slightly, and cupped her breasts.

'You're lovely,' he murmured, and she felt his fingers close gently and squeeze, just slightly. 'So beautiful. I want you, Ronnie,' he whispered, his breath soft against her skin, and his mouth lowered and brushed over one straining nipple.

She cried out and arched against him, and he scooped her up and laid her on the bed, coming down beside her and drawing her nipple into his mouth greedily.

She cried out again, shocked by the sharp stab of desire that shot through her as he suckled deeply on her breast. He switched to the other one, unable to get enough of her, and then his hand was touching her, testing her readiness, stroking her to a wild frenzy.

'Nick,' she sobbed, and he moved over her, covering her with his body, entering her with one swift stroke that brought her to a wild, shuddering climax in his arms.

He followed her seconds later, and this time the tears wouldn't be held in check. He didn't know. He dropped his head into her shoulder, his breath rasping, his heart pounding against hers as she struggled not to cry out loud, and then he shifted so that his weight was off her chest but their bodies were still intimately entwined, neither of them able to let go, too exhausted to move any further.

I love you! she wanted to say, but she knew she couldn't. Not now, with the spectre of Anna looming over them, and maybe not ever. And so she lay in the dimly lit room, the tears drying on her cheeks, and wondered if it would get easier, or if she'd feel this terrible pain of loving Nick every time he touched her.

After a while they grew cold, and he turned out the light and drew the quilt over them. She shivered, and he pulled her into his arms and loved her again and again through the night.

And then the cold fingers of dawn crawled over the horizon, and Ronnie woke with a start to the unaccustomed tenderness of a body well loved, and the sound of her alarm clock on the other side of the wall.

'Oh, my God,' she muttered, and, dropping a feather-soft kiss on his hair, she slid out of bed, dived into her dress and fled downstairs. She found her shoes under his trousers in the middle of the hall floor, and her coat and bag dropped just inside the door.

There was no time to leave him a note, but he would know where she'd gone, and she daren't wake him again or she'd never get to work!

She eased the door open, hoping there would be no one about at six-thirty on a Sunday morning, and as she stepped onto her path she noticed her car window was open a crack and it was just starting to rain. She opened the door, wound it up and shut the door, just as a battered old car pulled up and the young lad from over the way was dropped off on the corner.

He jogged up the path, did a mild double take at Ronnie's evening dress and unbrushed hair, and grinned.

'I won't tell if you don't,' he called softly, and, flushing to the roots of her hair, she shot through her front door and clicked it shut behind her. At least he hadn't seen her come out of Nick's house!

Ten minutes later she was showered, her make-up was off and replaced with masses of concealer to cover the whisker burn and the dark shadows under her eyes. A pale lipstick to cover the soft, rosy blush of much-kissed lips, and she was in her uniform and out the door.

The sound of a car woke Nick, and he stretched and turned over—and remembered. His eyes flew open, but she was gone, only the lingering scent of her skin left to remind him of the night that had passed.

Dear God, she was lovely. Warm, soft, willing—his body reacted to the memory, and he groaned and rolled onto his front. How could he feel like this still, after—what? Four, five times?

'You've got a lot of catching up to do,' he reminded himself, and jackknifed out of bed to see if she'd left him a note downstairs.

He found nothing except her tights, shredded by his eager hands, and his hastily shed shoes and trousers, lying on the hall floor. His briefs were on the bottom stair, and the kitchen lights were still on from last night.

He scooped up his clothes, leaned against the wall and laughed, just with the joy of being alive. It had been wonderful. Making love to Ronnie had been everything he could have hoped for and more.

Much more.

His smile faded, and he sat down on the bottom step with a bump. What was he supposed to tell the children? He couldn't have a discreet affair with her when she lived next door, for heaven's sake! And, anyway, he couldn't expose the kids to any more hurt.

Still, they'd be moving soon. It would be easier then to be discreet—except that Meg and Jimmy might see them creeping around.

He knew that being open and telling the children about him and Ronnie was out of the question. If he ever decided to get married again, and he couldn't believe he would, then he'd tell them. For now, though, this affair with Ronnie had to be kept from them, and from their friends and neighbours, because it would get back to them at school, he was sure.

A secret, he remembered, was something you only told one person at a time.

So, no secrets.

A dull ache in the region of his heart caught him by surprise. Odd. It felt curiously like grief.

Shaking his head to clear it, he ran upstairs, stripped his sheets and put them in the machine, remade the bed and had a shower. Then he tidied up all trace of

Ronnie's visit, hung the sheets out on the line and sat down.

It was hours before he was due to pick up the children, but suddenly he needed to see them, to connect with them, to remind himself of how much he loved them.

He glanced at his watch. Mid-morning. Peter would be in church already, about to take the family service, but Clare and the children might still be in the house. He reached for the phone.

'Hello, darling,' Anna's mother said, sounding friendly and welcoming and making him feel guilty. 'You've just caught us, we were on our way over to the church. I was saying to Peter, it's ages since you've come for lunch. I don't suppose you want to come over, do you? It would be lovely to hear all about your new job and the house.'

'I'll bring the details,' he said, and hung up, humming softly. He didn't need Ronnie—and she certainly didn't need him with all his problems and hang-ups.

He was in the car in less than two minutes.

CHAPTER FIVE

RONNIE didn't see Nick until Monday, and then it was in the usual chaos of the ward. She'd gone home on Sunday afternoon to find he was out, and he didn't come back with the children until nearly nine, after she'd crawled into bed, exhausted.

She'd half hoped he'd left her a note, but there was nothing. She even pulled up the mat in the hall to see if it had drifted underneath—highly unlikely, but she was clutching at straws. Then they came home, and she slipped on her dressing-gown and sat downstairs, hoping he'd ring the doorbell, but he didn't, and in the end she crept back upstairs and lay in her bed, so close to him, and longed for his touch.

And then on Monday, when she was prepping pre-ops, he came in during what she imagined was his coffee-break and tracked her down.

'Ronnie.'

Just the one word, saying nothing really. His eyes gave nothing away, nor did his tone. Her heart sank.

'Morning,' she said brightly. 'All well?'

'Yes—um, fine. Look, Ronnie, can we have a word?'

'What, now? I'm up to my eyes,' she said quietly. 'How about later?'

But later didn't happen. She didn't get a lunch-break because one of Oliver's post-ops started to haemorrhage and had to go back up to Theatre, which took any time she might have scraped up.

Nick came onto the ward later and caught her eye, but she shook her head. She was too busy—a patient's relatives needed to talk to her about taking their mother home and dealing with her colostomy, and she was setting up an appointment for them to talk to the stoma nurse and have the management of her condition explained.

And that evening, of course, the children were about.

He rang her doorbell later on, about nine-thirty, after the house had gone quiet, but he didn't come right in, instead just hovered in the doorway.

'I can't leave the kids,' he explained in a low voice. 'I just needed to talk to you about the other night.'

He seemed distant, a little reserved, and her sinking heart slid a little farther down into her boots. 'What about it?' she said, trying to muster a little calm.

'We didn't—um—it was a bit unexpected. I wasn't prepared for it. I wanted to know if there was any chance you might be pregnant, but I assume you're on the Pill?'

Ronnie laughed, a hollow, humourless little sound that rang in the empty hall. 'Why would I be on the Pill, Nick? It was the first time.'

His brow creased in puzzlement. 'The fir— You mean—' He broke off, looking stunned. 'Ronnie?'

She shrugged. 'It's no big deal. It had to happen some time. It's not exactly a major issue—well, not any more.'

He glanced around, then stepped inside, pushing her back into the hall and closing the door softly. 'You were a *virgin*?' he said incredulously, his eyes locked on hers. She nodded, and his face softened. 'My God, Ronnie—why didn't you say something?'

'Such as what? Like I said, it had to happen some

time, and it doesn't seem to be such a big deal any more.'

'I had no idea. Oh, Ronnie, I'm sorry…'

'Don't be sorry. Just be nice to me.'

That slipped out without her permission, but it seemed to do the trick. With a ragged groan he drew her into his arms and hugged her gently. 'Oh, sweetheart. I wish I'd known, I would have made it special for you.'

She laughed into his shoulder. 'It *was* special. It was a wonderful evening, and a natural conclusion.'

'And I didn't do anything to protect you. Damn.' He cupped her shoulders and held her back, looking down into her eyes. 'Ronnie, are you likely to conceive at this time?'

She shook her head. 'No. I've just had a period— literally just. I'm safe for a few days.'

His shoulders seemed to drop. 'Thank God, because the morning-after pill has a lousy success rate if you leave it too long.' He paused, shifting uncomfortably, then raised his head again and met her eyes. 'Look, Ronnie, we've got to talk about this. It's the kids— I don't want them knowing about us. They've been through so much, and if they think there's any chance we'll get together they'll just get hurt again, and I can't let that happen. They have to come before us.'

The words fell like stones on her heart. He seemed so sure they had no future—and on Saturday night he'd cried for Anna. Maybe he wasn't really over her. Maybe his grief and guilt and love wouldn't let him go, in which case there was no chance for them.

'They don't have to know,' she assured him, trying not to cry out loud.

'If it happens again, they'll find out. What if someone sees us creeping around?'

Like the teenager on Sunday morning, Ronnie
thought with a little flicker of dismay, and knew he
was right. Nothing could happen as long as they were
living next to each other and the children were around.

'So is this goodbye?' she whispered unsteadily.

His arms tightened around her convulsively. 'No,'
he denied. 'I need you, Ronnie. I felt whole again on
Saturday for the first time in years. I just don't see how
we can work it—and I can't contemplate meeting you
in a hotel or anything like that. It's too sordid.'

'But we can still see each other when the children
are about. I work with you, I live next door—we can
spend time together if we're careful to keep it casual.'
Did she sound as desperate as she felt?

'You can help me with the house. Maybe there…'

Her heart, clutching at straws, soared with hope.
'Maybe. I'm sure we can work something out—'

'Daddy?'

He straightened, his head coming up and his arms
dropping as he moved towards the door. 'Amy's calling. I have to go.'

She followed him, stopping him for a second and
going up on tiptoe to press a quick kiss to his lips.
'Knock on the wall and I'll bring you coffee out to the
garden,' she suggested, and he laughed a little sadly.

'At least the fence will keep us in order. And,
Ronnie? Thanks for Saturday. You're right, it *was* special.'

And then he was gone, the door clicking softly shut
behind him.

Ronnie wandered into the sitting room to wait for

his knock, and curled up in a chair, thinking about what he'd said.

It was both better and worse than it might have been, she supposed. Better, in that he hadn't said it had been a mistake and mustn't happen again at all costs, and worse, because he seemed so convinced their love was doomed to failure.

If it *was* love on his part. It certainly was on hers, at least. there was no doubt in her heart about that.

She sat there in the dark, listening to the murmured voices and occasional footsteps next door, and finally, at about ten-thirty, there was a quiet knock on the wall.

She opened the garden door and stepped out, hugging herself against the cold. 'Hi,' she said softly.

'Hi. Sorry to be so long. Amy wouldn't settle.'

'I heard. Is she OK now?'

'I think so.'

A little voice drifted out on the night. 'Daddy? Who are you talking to?'

He sighed. 'It's Ronnie,' he called softly.

'Is she here?'

He sighed again, and she could picture his resignation on the other side of the fence. 'Forget the coffee,' he said heavily. 'I'll see you tomorrow.'

''Night,' she murmured. 'Sleep well.'

There was a soft snort, and the click of his latch. She looked up at the stars, and the crystals of ice along the top of the fence, and realised it was a bitterly cold night.

She went back inside, suddenly aware of how cold her feet were in their thin socks. She made a coffee and went up to bed, and lay there, her head inches from Nick's headboard, and missed him.

*   *   *

'Mr Sarazin?'

Nick looked up, to see Sue Warren, his fledgling SHO, hurrying towards him. 'Sorry to call you out of Theatre. She's in cubicle three—she's been brought in by ambulance direct. Her neighbour found her lying in bed, looking very shocked. I think she might have a ruptured bowel.'

'Why?' he asked, forcing himself to concentrate on Sue and not on his thoughts of Ronnie.

'Her abdomen's rigid, she's in a lot of pain, she's got a history of constipation and rectal blood loss, her temperature's 40°C, there's free gas on her abdo film—'

Nick nodded and pushed the curtain aside, moving towards the frail, elderly woman on the bed. 'Do we have a name for her?'

'Winnie Eddison.'

'Winnie?' He bent over the semi-conscious patient, taking her hand and squeezing it gently. 'Winnie, can you hear me? My name's Nick Sarazin—I'm going to have a quick look at your tummy.'

He scanned her as he spoke, noticing the profuse sweating and obvious pain. 'How long have you been feeling sore, Winnie?' he asked her.

She moaned. 'Oh, ages. I was a bit worried about the blood—it seemed a bit much for piles.'

Nick frowned. 'I'm just going to have a listen.' He ran the stethoscope over her abdomen, but it was ominously silent. Glancing up, he saw the X-rays on the light-box and nodded. 'OK. Right, we need to take her up now. Winnie, I'm going to have to have a look inside your tummy and find out what's making you so ill, OK? Do you understand?'

She nodded weakly, clutching at him with thin, bird-like fingers. 'Am I going to be all right?' she asked.

'I hope so. I think you've got a little hole in your bowel, and we need to find out why and sort it out. Right, everybody, let's get her under way. I want two units of blood cross matched, FBC, U and E, blood sugar and amylase, and let's get some saline into her, stat. She'll need a nasogastric tube to empty her stomach, and we'll start her on ampicillin, gentamicin and metronidazole IV. Has she had any pain relief?'

'No,' Sue told him. 'I wanted you to see her first.'

'Right, I've seen her. Let's get 2.5 mg morphine into her IV with 12.5 mg stemetil intramuscularly—now, please. It's all right, Winnie, we'll soon have you feeling better. I'll see you upstairs in a minute.'

He left the bustle in Resus and headed towards Theatre, to warn them and to scrub again. She was frail, she was elderly, she was in a bad way and he didn't want his promise that she would soon be better to be in vain.

They had yet to divine the cause of her perforation, of course. It might be that there was something very simple, or he might have to take out a large section of bowel or give her a temporary colostomy to rest part of it until it recovered. Or it might be much, much worse.

Only time would tell. He rang Ronnie from the theatre and warned her to stand by, giving her all the details he could. 'I don't know about relatives. They said something about a daughter—she might get directed up to you. I'll keep in touch if there's any news.'

'OK. I'll speak to you later.'

'Fine.' He glanced round, but there was no one there.

'What are you doing for lunch?' he asked under his breath.

Ronnie laughed, a soft, musical sound that made his gut clench. 'What's that?' she said wryly. 'We're up to our eyeballs here.'

He was conscious of disappointment, but then Winnie Eddison pushed herself back into the forefront of his mind. 'I have to go. I may not be through here anyway. I'll ring you.'

He scrubbed, finishing just as Winnie was brought in and the anaesthetist took over.

'Right, she's all yours,' he said, and Nick looked at Sue.

'Ever done one of these?'

She shook her head.

'Right. If she was younger or you'd done it before, I'd let you tackle it. As it is, watch carefully and keep your hands clean. I might let you do a bit if you're good.'

He caught Kate's eye and grinned. He and Kate were all right now. He'd spoken to her, told her he wasn't her type and she'd settled down into an easy bantering relationship which he could live with.

He held out his hand and she slapped a scalpel precisely into his palm. He thought it was a good job she wasn't a vindictive shrew, or that might have been the end of his surgical career.

'Right, we want a nice big incision so we can see what's happening, but we don't have to go mad. Let's find out what her problem is.'

Ronnie picked up the phone to find Nick on the other end, and gave a sigh of relief. 'How is it? You've been ages. Her daughter's frantic.'

'Sorry. She's OK. She had a very messy threadbare bowel. She's obviously had diverticular disease for years, and she's been neglecting it. I've had to remove about half of her colon and give her a permanent co-lostomy, unfortunately, but I'd say she was lucky her neighbour found her. I don't think she would have lasted much longer.'

'Is she coming to us or going to ITU?'

He snorted. 'What do you think? She's only got raging peritonitis and massive blood loss.'

'Oh, a day case, then,' Ronnie joked, and Nick snorted at the other end of the line.

'I'll see you later—she'll be with you in about half an hour. I have to go back to my list. Anyone prepped and ready?'

'Only about four. I'll warn them you're under way again.'

And that was how Wednesday went on. Thursday wasn't much better, and then she finally had a day off.

A long weekend, in fact. She could always go down to Southampton and visit her father, but a tiny bit of her about a mile wide wanted to stay put in case Nick had time to notice she was alive.

Then, on Friday night, when she'd cleaned the house from top to bottom, done her shopping and was about to start on a pile of ironing, he knocked on her door, children in tow, and dangled some keys under her nose. 'I've got the house.'

'It's yours?' she asked, and then without thinking she hugged him, pulling back almost as soon as she touched him because she remembered she wasn't supposed to do it. Then she looked down at the children and grinned. 'How exciting! Are you going over there now?'

'We're going to have a pizza picnic on the floor,' Ben told her.

'I want chicken and mushroom pie,' Amy began, and Nick hugged her against his side.

'You can have chicken and mushroom pie, sweetheart,' he assured her, and then met Ronnie's eyes again. 'Um—we wondered, if you're not doing anything, if you wanted to join us. After all, we wouldn't have found it without you, so you ought to be there to celebrate.'

She tried to be practical and not allow herself to drown in the smoky depths of his eyes. 'Isn't the power off?' she said doubtfully, looking round at the gathering dusk.

He chuckled. 'Oh, yes, and it will be freezing in the house, but I'm taking a few candles and I thought we might light a fire.'

It sounded like fun—much more fun than her ironing. 'I'll grab my coat,' she said, and ran to fetch it, scooping up a packet of biscuits on the way. 'Anything else I should bring?'

'Just yourself,' he told her, and she wasn't sure if she imagined it or if there was real warmth in his voice.

The journey was very short—so short it was hardly worth getting in the car, but it was cold and dark and, anyway, they had to get the pizza—and the pie!

The children were fizzing with excitement, and so was Ronnie. She'd hardly had a moment to speak to Nick except on the ward, and it had always been hurried, always about patients and always frustrating! Now he'd invited her to join them, and she wondered how much coercion he'd had from the children, and how much of the invitation had come from him.

'I'm sitting on the window-seat!' Ben yelled, pelting

into the house past them and going straight to the bottom of the 'tower' rooms.

Amy ran after him, protesting, and Nick and Ronnie followed more slowly. 'There are five window-seats— I don't think we have to rush,' he said drily. He put the bags down on the middle seat, spread out a rug on the floor and set out all the picnic paraphernalia in the middle.

They were able to see reasonably well because of the streetlights outside, and so he didn't have to bother with the candles, to Ronnie's relief. She could just picture Ben charging past and knocking one over, starting a fire.

There was a big pizza box, a paper-wrapped pie for Amy, four glasses, a carton of juice and a bottle of wine.

'Alky-free, I'm afraid, but I'm driving,' Nick said with an apologetic grin.

'I'm quite happy with that,' Ronnie assured him. 'Can I do anything?'

'Eat,' he said, and the children slithered off the window-seats and dived into the pizza box.

'Hey, you've got a pie!' Ben yelled, and Amy started to cry.

'She can have a bit of pizza, too, if she wants,' Nick said, and Amy stuck her tongue out. Ronnie said nothing, but wondered how much Amy didn't like pizza and how much she wanted the extra attention of having to have a pie as well.

Hmm.

She caught Amy's eye just as she took a huge bite of pizza, and the girl looked uncomfortable for a second. Ronnie stifled a smile. So, she was just playing games with her dad. How like a little girl.

'Are you going to try the fire?' she asked Nick as they munched.

'It's cold,' Amy said, shivering and unwrapping her pie, her little legs sticking out from under the paper. She looked like a little doll, sitting bolt upright with her legs out straight as only children were flexible enough to do.

'Yeah, light the fire, Dad,' Ben urged. 'It'll be really cool to have a fire.'

Ronnie nearly laughed. Cool, to have a fire? Still, never mind the strange phraseology, it was lovely to see them both so excited. She tore up the pizza box and crumpled up Amy's pie paper, while Nick took a torch and brought in some coal from the coal bunker by the back door.

'Here we go—a fire.' Then he patted his pockets a little helplessly, and looked at Ronnie. 'I don't suppose you've got matches?'

Ronnie fished in her bag and brought out a cheap plastic cigarette lighter, one of those disposable gas ones. 'Here—this any good?'

Nick took it thoughtfully. 'I didn't know you smoked.'

'I don't. My car-door lock freezes up sometimes. I always carry it in the winter.'

'How resourceful.' He flicked the wheel, and held the flame to the crumpled paper in the grate. As it caught and started to blaze, Ronnie wondered belatedly when the chimney had last been swept. There were flecks of soot on the floor by the grate, and more in the grate itself.

If it was blocked, of course, it wouldn't draw…

The cardboard box caught, greasy from the cheese,

and within moments the room was filled with billowing smoke.

Oops!

They started to cough, and Nick took the carton of juice and threw it at the fire, dousing the flames in a great steaming sizzle.

'Chimney's blocked,' he wheezed, and caught Ronnie's eye. She was laughing—she couldn't help herself, and nor could the children, and then Nick joined in, sagging back against the marble surround and laughing till tears streamed down his face.

'I'll open the window,' he gasped after a moment, and pushed one of the casements up to slide the catch across. As he released it, it crashed down, the sash cords broken, and the glass shattered all over the garden outside.

There was a second of stunned silence, then he swore, quietly and very mildly but with considerable feeling.

Ben wagged his finger. 'Swear-box, Daddy,' he said virtuously, and Nick rolled his eyes.

'I'll go outside and push it up—Ronnie, could you push the catch across for me? And I'll have to find some board and seal it up. Blast.'

He stomped outside, and Ronnie and the children started to giggle.

'What?' he said, standing outside in the garden, his hands on his hips, glowering at them through the window. 'What now?'

Ronnie shook her head, biting the inside of her lip, and stood up. 'Nothing. Shut the window.'

He harrumphed and stepped up to the outside of the window, and glass crunched under his feet.

'You'll have to clear that up so cats don't cut them-

selves on it,' Ronnie advised, and earned herself another dirty look through the shattered pane as he
slammed the window up. Oops! Somebody was in a
grump! She slipped the catch across, pulled out a loose
piece of glass and handed it to him through the hole.

'Here—another bit for the pile.'

'So kind.'

He stomped back inside, grinding to a halt when
Ronnie yelled at him, 'Shoes!'

'What about them?'

'They'll be full of glass.'

He muttered something that Ben didn't hear, or there
would have been another contribution to the swear-box,
and marched into the room in socks.

'Anybody got any other ideas?' he asked drily, and
Ronnie handed him a glass of wine.

'Yes—drink this and relax. I know it's unleaded—
just pretend.'

He gave a weary gust of laughter and took the glass,
dropping down beside her on his haunches. 'Come
round the house with me while these two finish off the
pizza and the biscuits. I want to tell you what I've
planned—and then we'll see if there's a bit of board
in the garden we can use to block up the window.'

He helped her to her feet, picked up the torch and
told the children to stay where they were. Then he took
her upstairs, right to the top, closed the attic door and
drew her into his arms in the dim glow from the streetlights. 'I've been wanting to do this all week,' he
sighed, and just as his mouth came down on hers, they
heard Amy's voice.

'Daddy? Daddy, I need a wee and I can't see the
loo!'

He groaned and laughed. 'Tomorrow. They're going

to Anna's parents in the morning, and staying for half-term. We'll come back tomorrow—and I'll sweep the chimneys and we can have a fire and a real picnic.'

He went down, and Ronnie looked around the gloomy attic. One room was still full of junk, and rolled up at one side was an old rug.

They could unroll it in front of the fire, she thought, and remembered all the films she'd seen with couples entwined in front of a fireplace, their bodies gilded by the dancing flames, and she wondered if that was what Nick had in mind, and if he'd think she was brazen to suggest it.

Whatever, just to be on the safe side, she'd nip into a chemist in the morning. There was no harm in being prepared!

'Stay for lunch,' Anna's mother coaxed.

Nick shook his head, feeling a little guilty. 'I want to get on with the house. The first thing I've got to do is fix a window, and then sweep the chimneys.'

'We had a fire, and it smoked all in the room, and Daddy threw orange juice on it to put it out!' Amy told her grandmother excitedly.

'Oh, darling, is it safe?' Clare asked worriedly. He nodded, laughing. 'Oh, it's safe. Richard's checked it for me. It just needs…a little work, that's all. Well, probably more than just a little,' he confessed. 'There's masses to do before the builders start, and I want to do as much as I can this weekend.'

'Well, be careful. Don't overdo it. You're looking tired.'

'I'm fine,' he assured her. 'Don't worry about me.'

'Ronnie can help you, Daddy,' Amy suggested.

'Who's Ronnie?' Peter asked.

'Um—my neighbour,' Nick said, being what Anna would have called frugal with the truth.

'How kind of him,' Clare said.

'He's not a him, he's a her,' Amy explained, and Nick avoided everyone's eyes and chuckled at Amy's grammar.

'I must get on—I need to get to the builders' merchants before they shut,' he said a little wildly.

'Well, have fun and keep in touch,' Clare said, eyeing him speculatively. He kissed her, and wondered if she could read his mind and realised that he just wanted to get back to Ronnie. Probably. Oh, damn.

It was lust, he told himself, temporary insanity. He'd get over it. Familiarity breeds contempt, he reminded himself. Given time, he'd lose interest. Not that he'd lost interest in Anna in over ten years. Still, that was different.

Wasn't it?

CHAPTER SIX

RONNIE had arranged to meet Nick at the house at eleven-thirty, after he'd dropped the children off with their grandparents.

There had been a sort of suppressed, guilty longing in his eyes as he'd asked her to spend the day with him, and she wondered if he felt guilty because of Anna's parents babysitting while he dallied with her, or if it was because of Anna, or if she'd just misunderstood.

She didn't have a clue. It could have been any of them, or a bit of each. Whatever, she didn't feel guilty, and she was having a lot of trouble being suppressed. She was *aching* to be alone with him again, even just to talk, to smile, to laugh without an audience of interested bystanders.

She rang the doorbell, a sort of metal knob that you pulled which made a great clanging down the hall in the bowels of the house. It was like something out of a horror movie, and she almost laughed.

She would have if she'd been able to breathe, but Nick opened the door and her jaw dropped. He was wearing a scruffy old shirt and jeans with holes in the knees, his face was smeared with soot and he looked about ten years younger and good enough to eat.

He propped himself in the doorway and grinned, boyish and grubby and gorgeous, and her breath eased out in a ragged chuckle. 'You remind me of Dick Van Dyke in *Mary Poppins*,' she teased, eyeing the delicious scruffiness of him. 'Or one of Fagin's little monsters in *Oliver*.'

'Fagin's little monsters.' He pretended to glare at her, but there was no malice in it. 'You wait,' he threatened. 'You get to do the clean-up. I've saved it especially for you.'

'Clean up what—you, or the fireplace?' she asked, following him into the tower room. Chimney rods and brushes were scattered about the floor, there was a heap of soot in the grate and more tramped over the floor, and she could only imagine how well it would have stuck to that orange juice he'd thrown on the fire last night!

He grinned, his teeth startlingly white against the soot on his face. 'Both,' he said slowly, and she felt heat run through her. 'In fact, let's clean up the fireplace together, and then we can clean up each other.'

'Let's not. It'll take a deep bath and half a bar of soap to shift that lot,' she said, tilting her head at him and trying hard not to think about cleaning him up, 'and there's no hot water here.'

He snorted softly. 'Wrong. The old gas geyser over the sink works, after a fashion. I'll open the window while it runs, and we can carry the water upstairs to the bathroom.'

'Isn't that a lot of effort?' Ronnie asked, clamping down on her hyperactive imagination. 'We could just go home—or use cold.'

He raised an eyebrow. 'I'm sick of cold showers at the moment,' he said huskily. 'I'm looking forward to a nice, hot bath—and there's lots of room in that one.'

Their eyes met, and heat seared between them. For a second Ronnie stood there, motionless, and then she managed to drag her eyes away. 'Ah—um—we'd better get cleared up here, then,' she croaked, and wondered where the self-possessed, sensible, unruffled Sister Matthews had gone.

Legged it, at the first sign of trouble, she thought with a quiet chuckle of despair, and looked around for a dustpan and brush.

It took them two hours to sweep the main chimney in the drawing room that overlooked the cloistered and secluded garden, and another hour to clear up the soot even vaguely.

It seemed to get everywhere, into every nook and cranny, and, as Nick said, there was precious little point in worrying about it, because the electrician and plumber were about to descend on Monday and make far more mess.

'I'm starving,' Ronnie announced as they stood back grubbily and admired their handiwork.

'Me, too. I've brought a picnic. Let's get cleaned up and we can eat.'

They didn't bother with the bath, because they couldn't find a bucket that didn't leak. Instead, they washed in the kitchen sink, swilling off their arms and hands and faces as well as they could. Then Nick took the flannel from her and dabbed at her cheek.

'You've got a streak still,' he said softly, and his voice was tender and a little gruff and Ronnie could have stood there forever with his hands dabbing gently at her face. He'd taken off his shirt, and she was only too aware of the breadth of his shoulders and the smoothness of his skin, gliding tautly over firm muscle and strong bone. A drop of water was slithering down his neck, over the hollow of his throat and down into the fine, dark hair in the centre of his chest. She wanted to catch it on her tongue, to lick the droplet away...

Then he dropped the flannel in the sink, cradled her face in his hands and pressed a simple, innocent kiss to her lips.

'I'm going to light the fire in the drawing room,' he murmured, and released her. 'There's an old rug up in the attic—you might try to bring it down and put it in front of the fireplace, so we can sit on it to eat.'

He tugged on a jumper instead of the sooty shirt and went out of the back door to fetch coal and wood and whatever for the fire.

She stood rooted to the spot for what seemed like an age, and then remembered to breathe again. That rug she'd had fantasies about! And a fire—oh, heavens!

She ran up to the attic, pulled the heavy rug out of the room and down the stairs, and looked at it. It was dusty and grubby, and needed a good thump. She dragged it out of the back door, just as Nick was coming back up the path with an armful of kindling.

'Want to help me bang the dust out of this?' she asked, and he gave her a slightly strained smile.

'Sure. I'll just put this in the fireplace and get it lit.'

Had she imagined the tension on his face? She didn't think so. What had happened to the easy camaraderie of earlier? And the light-hearted flirtation? The shared bath, for heaven's sake! Her heart sank and she forced herself to concentrate on being sensible. 'Want my lighter?'

He shook his head. 'I've got matches. I'm a good boy scout today.'

So was she, Ronnie thought, remembering the condoms in her bag and forgetting all about being sensible. Well, that sort of sensible, anyway. Colour ran into her cheeks, and she reminded herself that they very likely wouldn't be needed anyway, with that look on his face. With a sigh she hoisted the rug over her shoulder and set off down the garden to find a suitable spot.

There was a washing line, sagging diagonally across the overgrown lawn, and Nick appeared just as she was struggling to flop the rug over it.

'Let me help,' he said, and took the other end, lifting it easily. He'd brought an old broom and, telling her to stand back, he thumped the broom into the middle of the rug. Dirt and dust flew, and she coughed and stepped back, happy to leave him to it.

After a few minutes he gave up, and tugged it off the line.

'That should do it,' he said, and draped it over his shoulder. 'Time for lunch.'

They ate in front of the fire which was now burning merrily in the drawing room, with a good view out over the tangled garden, and the February sun poured in and warmed them from the other side. Ronnie thought it would have been perfect if there hadn't been that strange tension between them which she couldn't quite fathom.

She hadn't imagined it earlier, when he'd passed her on the path, and it had got worse. She didn't know why it had suddenly sprung up, but it was almost as if he was nervous. She had a funny feeling he was going to tell her something she didn't want to hear.

Then Nick caught her eye, and everything seemed to tilt on its axis and slide quietly into another dimension. 'OK?' he asked softly, and she nodded.

'Time for dessert,' he said, and reached into the cool-box. He held up a strawberry, fat and ripe and hopelessly out of season but all the more delicious for it, and she bit into it and juice ran down over her lips.

He ate the other half, then leaned forward and caught the dribble of juice on her chin with his tongue just before she wiped it away. Her breath jammed in her throat, but he didn't kiss her. He just fed her another strawberry, and then another, each time catching the juice with an elusive sweep of his tongue, until she was ready to scream with frustration.

Finally, he swept the picnic aside and moved closer, kneeling in front of the fire and drawing her up into his arms so that they knelt face to face.

Then, and only then, did he kiss her, and she thought her bones would melt with the tender onslaught of his mouth and the relief of knowing that he still wanted her.

She could still taste strawberries on his lips, sweet and fresh and somehow wickedly exotic, and she closed her eyes and sighed against him. This was where she belonged, she thought vaguely. Here, with Nick, in his arms, making what was surely love.

Common sense resurrected itself, and she looked past him to the window. 'Isn't this a bit dangerous?' she asked, looking out into the garden. 'We might be seen.'

'The gate's locked, and there are no houses overlooking us.' He trailed a finger down her cheek, under her chin and down to the buttons of her shirt, slipping the first one free. 'No one's going to see us.'

He was right. She stopped worrying and concentrated on Nick.

And Nick, being the good boy scout he'd promised, remembered what she'd forgotten yet again so there would be no unforeseen consequences.

She felt sad, with that tiny scrap of her brain that still had independent function, but she knew he was right. There were already too many complications, even if her body did cry out to bear his child.

Not now, she told herself, and maybe not ever, but for now at least she had him, and the flickering flames of a real fire, and the fading warmth of the afternoon sun sinking behind the lilac at the end of the overgrown garden.

And then she stopped thinking about anything except the power of his body locked with hers, and the feel of his skin, and the sensation welling in her until it fractured into a thousand fragments and sent her tumbling into heaven.

Ronnie ached from end to end. Two days of clearing up soot, ripping off wallpaper and scrubbing out the insides of the kitchen cupboards while Nick stripped the paint on the doors had left her tired, stiff and yet curiously exhilarated.

Or was that because of the little sorties to the drawing room, to picnic and make love on the ancient rug, surrounded by the secrecy of the garden and cocooned in the warmth of the fire?

Either. Both. Whatever the cause, she was finding Monday morning back at work a little hard to cope with. They'd settled into an easy camaraderie over the weekend, and Ronnie wondered how Nick would behave towards her in front of their colleagues.

They'd been seen at the ball plastered all over each other on the dance floor, so there surely wouldn't be any surprises to anyone if they were seen together. Of course they'd be professional, and there'd be no stolen kisses in the sluice or quick cuddles in the kitchen, she thought regretfully, but maybe he'd smile that special smile, or say something quietly to make her pulse race and her cheeks heat.

Heaven knows, just seeing him, it would probably be enough to do that!

And yet when she did there was no time to worry about what they'd done at the weekend or how they would react to each other in public, because he had just come onto the ward when he was bleeped.

'May I?' Nick asked, heading for her office.

'Be my guest.'

Ronnie followed him, hoping for a quiet word, but his manner alerted her professional instincts, and she eavesdropped shamelessly. He straightened, looked at her with growing dismay in his eyes and snapped out a few questions.

'Send him up now—just get him stabilised enough to move and send him straight to Theatre. I'll go and scrub—yeah, I'm on the ward now. I'll tell them.'

He put the phone down and ran his hand over his hair. 'That was A and E. Ryan O'Connor's been stabbed by a patient.'

Ronnie felt her blood run cold. 'Oh, my God. I'll get a room ready.'

'Don't hurry. It sounds as if he might not make it. I've changed my mind, I'm going down there—I might have to open him up in Resus. I don't know if we've got time to move him. Ring and tell them, would you? I'll be in touch.'

And he left, his long stride eating up the floor, and once through the doors she heard him break into a run. It must be serious, she thought numbly. Poor Ryan. She'd only met the gentle Canadian A and E consultant a few times, but he'd impressed her with his kindness and warmth, and he was very highly thought of professionally.

What a great loss it would be if some random act of violence wiped him out just like that, without warning.

She thought of Ginny, his wife of two years, and wondered if she knew, and how they would tell her.

And then she wondered how she'd feel if it was Nick, and she felt cold all the way to her heart. It was then, at that moment, that she realised how much she loved him.

'Chest saw,' Nick rapped out, and it was in his hand before he'd finished speaking. My God, he thought moments later, looking at the blood pouring into the cavity in front of him. 'Suction!'

Again they were there almost before he asked, a well-orchestrated team, working without thought, without hesitation, on one of their number, fighting for him as they would for anyone, but with that extra edge of commitment and determination. Nobody was going to give up on this man—nobody!

'Pressure's dropping,' the anaesthetist warned, and the nurse who was bagging in the blood as fast as she could squeezed even faster.

'We need another vein—someone do a cutdown on his ankle and get another line in fast, please. I can't see where this leak is.'

He took the sucker from the nurse and swept the area, watching like a hawk for any hint of where the blood might be coming from.

'Got it,' he said finally and, reaching into Ryan's chest, he grabbed the offending vessel. 'Right, let's sew this one up and look for the others.'

It took hours, tackling the main leaks in A and E

and then transferring him to Theatre for some slow, thorough searching to make sure all the leaks had been found and every vessel repaired. Amazingly, Ryan's heart had been missed, but his lungs and pulmonary vessels had been badly damaged, and Nick was still very concerned.

'He'll need to go to ITU,' he said, and was greeted with a wry snort from the anaesthetist.

'Not a chance. They're chock-a-block. Didn't you hear the news last night? There was a bad accident on the A14—some went to Addenbrookes, others to Ipswich, some here. ITU is already overstretched.'

Nick wiped his face on his shoulder and sighed. 'I can't just send him to the ward—unless Ronnie can get extra staff. He'll need qualified specialling for at least twenty-four hours.'

'Ring her.'

Nick nodded, his head still bent over Ryan's chest, scanning the surgical field for leaks and any other cuts he might have missed. Finally satisfied that there were none, he closed the chest wall and straightened. It was four-thirty—six and a half hours, give or take, since they'd started.

His stomach rumbled, and he stretched his neck and rolled his head on his shoulders. 'OK, let's take him through to Recovery and look after him there for a little while—I'll ring Ronnie and talk to her about a bed, and I suppose I ought to speak to his wife.'

'She's waiting outside.'

That comment was from Matt Jordan, the other A and E consultant, who had stood quietly at the back for the past hour without interruption. Nick turned to look at him, tugging down his mask and snapping off the blood-streaked gloves. 'I'll talk to her.'

'I'll come with you, if you like. I know her pretty well.'

'How is she?'

Matt raised an eyebrow. 'How would you be?'

Nick grinned. 'About that good, I suspect.'

Actually, she was holding up very well—until they went out there and told her that Ryan had come through the operation and had a chance. Then she seemed to crumple, first her face, then the rest of her body, and Matt caught her against his chest and hugged her, cradling her gently.

'That's right, you let go. You're a brave girl. Well done,' he murmured, and Nick left them alone. She was in good hands. He could speak to her in a minute. Just for now, he wanted to talk to Ronnie—and not only about their patient.

He just needed to connect with her, and it was a need he didn't like to examine too closely. He rang ITU first just to confirm the anaesthetist's prediction that they were full, then stabbed in the number of the ward extension. Ronnie picked up on the second ring.

'Surgical, Sister Matthews speaking.'

'Ronnie, it's Nick. We've just sent him through to Recovery.'

He could almost feel her sigh of relief. 'Well done,' she said, and she sounded a little choked. 'How is he?'

'Not good. I've plugged all the leaks but I had to open his chest in Resus. He's a mess, but I'm hoping he'll pull through. ITU, though, are over-full and can't take him. I'll keep him up here for a while, but then he'll have to come down to you. Is there anyone who can special him?'

'I'll do it,' she said without hesitation.

'But you've been on duty all day.'

'That's all right. There's no one else available at such short notice that I'd trust with him. I'll go home now, sleep till midnight and then come in. He can stay there till then, can't he?'

'Yes. I'll hang around here, just in case he springs another leak.'

'There's a duty room off the ward—it may not be in use. You could sleep there,' she suggested.

It sounded ideal. At least that way he could be within reach and still be fit to do his job tomorrow. 'I'll give you my keys and you can bring some stuff back with you so I don't have to look like a street bum in the morning.'

She laughed, a warm, sexy chuckle. 'I think you'd make a lovely street bum,' she teased, and he laughed.

'Thanks, Ronnie. I'll see you in a minute. I'll just check up on him and I'll come down and go over his notes with you. I imagine you'll have company most of the night—I expect his wife will stay beside him.'

'That's fine,' Ronnie assured him. 'She's a doctor, anyway. She won't be a problem.'

He hung up, curiously reluctant to break the connection, and cradled the phone tiredly. He still had hours of work to get through before he could even think about lying down, but right now he needed a short break. He checked that Ryan was stable and looking good, and then, without bothering to change, he headed down to the surgical ward—and Ronnie.

'Long day?' she commiserated, searching Nick's face with eyes all the sharper for loving him.

He grinned, a wry, tip-tilted grin with little humour and a lot of exhaustion, and nodded. 'I thought we were going to lose him,' he confessed. 'We couldn't find the leak, and every time we found one, he was leaking from somewhere else. It was a nightmare.'

'How's he looking now?' she asked, heading automatically for the kitchen and the kettle.

'Rough, but alive. Better than he did six hours ago.'

'I'll bet.' He was jiggling something in his pocket, and she held out her hand. 'Got your house keys?'

He dropped them in her palm. 'I forgot.'

He looked exhausted with the strain, and she tried to imagine what it must be like to come in new to an organisation and have everyone watch you struggle to save the life of a colleague. Talk about stress! 'What do you want—pyjamas? Wash stuff? Clean underwear?'

He grinned. 'Yeah—and a shirt, if you can find a clean one that doesn't need ironing.'

'I'll do my best.' She slid a cup of tea across the worktop to him and cradled her own mug thoughtfully. 'So, how long do you expect him to remain critical?'

'Hopefully, not long. The first twenty-four hours will be the worst. After that he should start to improve, but the greatest danger is clotting. His chest is like a colander—if we give him too much anticoagulant, he'll just leak all over again. If we don't, he'll clot. Catch-22.'

'So you'll juggle.'

He nodded. 'And let's just hope I don't drop the balls.'

He drained his tea, hot as it was, and put the mug down. 'I'm going back up. I'll see you later. Want me to give you a wake-up call?'

She smiled with relief. 'Would you? I might sleep through the alarm—or else not go to sleep in case I do!'

He chuckled. 'I know the feeling. You go to bed and sleep, princess,' he said softly. 'I'll wake you at eleven-thirty.'

And then he leaned over, pressed a quick, firm kiss to her lips and went.

CHAPTER SEVEN

'WAKEY-WAKEY, rise and shine!'

Ronnie groaned and rolled over, burying her face in the pillow. Nick was too darned chirpy for that time of night.

'Ronnie? Ronnie, wake up.'

''Mawake,' she mumbled into the receiver, and forced herself to sit up, pushing the hair back off her face and blinking in the dim light from the streetlamps. 'How is he?'

'Hanging on. Doesn't look wonderful. I keep bullying ITU, but they haven't got anything imminent. How soon can you get here?'

'I'm on my way,' she promised, sliding out of bed and standing up, just to make sure she didn't succumb to the urge to snuggle back down in the warm covers and slither off to oblivion again. 'Give me fifteen minutes and I'll be with you.'

She washed hastily, in tepid water to wake her up a little more, threw on a clean uniform and headed for the door. She was hungry, but she could make some toast on the ward. It wasn't a problem. She was on the ward in fourteen minutes, and rang Recovery to tell them she was in.

Five minutes later the rumble of wheels on the corridor warned her their patient was arriving, and Ryan was wheeled in and reattached to the waiting monitors. The night sister on duty came in and chatted for a moment, and then, once they were happy everything was working properly and he was stable after his transfer, she went.

'You made it, well done,' Nick said softly as she left.

'Of course. I said I'd be here.'

He grinned. 'So you did.'

'Where's Ginny?' Ronnie asked. 'Did she have to go home?'

He shook his head. 'No, I've sent her for something to eat—she hasn't had anything all day. The kids are with Matt and Sarah Jordan. They're at the same school or something and live just round the corner, so it's easy. I think Sarah's going to bring them in to see her in the morning. Where is she going to sleep?'

Ronnie thought how she'd feel, and knew the answer. 'Beside him—if she sleeps at all. I could bring in a little cot, but if he arrests or haemorrhages we could waste precious seconds moving it out of the way, so I think she'd better stay in the chair. They're pretty comfortable. She won't be the first person to have done it.'

'Or the last,' he said softly, looking down at Ryan.

'Tell me about him.'

Nick handed her the slim volume of notes off the end of the bed. 'Here are the details. I'm really more worried about things we might have missed than things we found, but as time goes by I think he might be lucky. Just watch his pressure and respirations like a hawk. Any sign of a pneumothorax, haemothorax, cardiac tamponade or any little gems like that, shout.'

Ronnie gave him a slight smile. 'Oh, don't you worry, I will. I put your stuff in the duty room,' she added, remembering how she'd felt, going through his drawers looking for clothes. She hadn't known where to find anything, and it was an odd feeling. It made her feel even more excluded in a way—after all, if she was a proper part of his life she'd know where he kept his pants and socks and shirts, and what type of toothpaste he used.

And there hadn't been an ironed shirt, so she'd taken one home and done it herself, quickly. It had felt frighteningly domestic, and she was well aware that she was only doing it to counteract the feeling of exclusion she'd had in his bedroom.

She forced herself to concentrate on Ryan O'Connor, but she was hungry and thirsty and Nick was just too close.

'How about some tea and toast?' she suggested.

He grinned. 'Sounds good. Who's going to make it?'

'Can I trust you with my patient?' she teased softly, and he chuckled.

'I think so, just about.'

So she left him with Ryan, went into the little kitchen and put the kettle on. The toaster swallowed four slices of bread with ease, and she leaned back against the worktop and wondered how she would cope with Nick just up the corridor, and if she'd be able to resist the urge to go in to him.

Thank God she was going to have to watch Ryan so closely! It might be the only thing to keep her sane.

The toast popped up and she buttered it generously. Never mind cholestrol, she thought. Tonight she needed comfort food, and hot buttered toast and tea would just hit the spot.

She took the tray back and found Nick making notes on the clipboard at the end of the bed.

'Problems?' she asked, setting the tray down on the locker.

'No. Just adjusting the dose of painkiller. He's got an automatic cylinder driver to deliver it, but he's bigger than I'd thought so I've upped the dose a touch. Can you adjust the pump?'

'Sure. Here, have some toast.' She altered the delivery rate on the infusion pump, and then sat down with her mug and a slice of dripping toast.

'Are you trying to kill me with heart disease?' he asked quizzically, and she grinned.

'Comfort food. There have to be some compensations for working all night and, let's face it, neither of us need to watch our weight.'

He chuckled softly, and took another slice. He didn't seem to mind, she thought, despite his words. There was something very companionable about sitting there in the dimly lit room, with nothing but the blip of the monitors and the soft, regular sound of Ryan's breathing to disturb them.

The nurses were going quietly about their duties, their feet almost silent on the shiny plastic floor, and, apart from the occasional groan from a patient in distress, there was nothing to distract her thoughts from Nick sitting there just across the bed, looking more tempting than he had any right to look after such a long day.

His jaw was heavily shadowed, his eyes red-rimmed and a little bloodshot, and he should have inspired her sympathy. Instead, she wanted nothing more than to drag him up the corridor to the privacy of the duty doctor's room and make love to him.

Apparently, it was mutual, she realised, catching his eye and surprising a look of longing there. 'Hello, foxy lady,' he said under his breath, and she felt her heart pick up and her skin colour softly.

Her lips parted slightly, and she closed her eyes and bent her head so she didn't have to look into those searing eyes and see what she couldn't have. At least, not now.

Ryan moaned softly, and instantly her head snapped up and she scanned the monitors automatically. His heart rate had picked up a little, but his blood pressure, measured by the central venous pressure line, was steady and constant.

'He's waking up,' Nick murmured. 'Damn, Ginny wanted to be here. Ryan? It's Nick Sarazin. How are you feeling?'

Ryan's eyes flickered open and he groaned again. 'Hurt,' he said, and tried to lick his lips. Ronnie tore open a pack of swabs and moistened his mouth with cool water. His eyes opened again and he tried to focus on her.

'Where am I?'

'Surgical ward—you had a fight in A and E.'

'Oh, Lord, yes,' he mumbled, and his eyes slid shut. 'So, what happened?' he slurred. 'My chest feels sawn in half.'

'It is,' Nick told him drily. 'I'm now intimately acquainted with the contents. He got your lungs and pulmonary vessels, but missed your heart. You're one lucky honcho.'

'I am?' he said with a weak smile. 'That's tough. Does that mean I'm going to live?'

'I'm afraid so.'

He said something rude under his breath, and Nick chuckled. 'I think you're definitely going to live. Ginny's just getting something to eat, she'll be back in a minute.'

He looked around, trying to focus, and frowned. 'Is this ITU?'

'No,' Ronnie told him. 'They didn't want you—too much trouble, they said. Staff are always difficult patients. They ask stupid questions and won't do as they're told, so they sent you to us.'

He chuckled, and then a spasm of pain crossed his features. 'Hell, you really did saw it up, didn't you?' he muttered after a moment. 'I always wondered what it felt like. Now I know, and I wish I didn't.' He said something else that would have had Ben reaching for the swear-box, and Ronnie wiped away the beads of sweat that formed on his brow.

He was propped up in the bed, his pillows carefully arranged to support his ribcage, and there was a long strip of gauze over the centre of his chest, covering the incision. The wound was sealed with plastic skin to prevent infection, but covered to prevent the sutures from catching on bedclothes. He was naked, of course, as were all post-operative patients of his severity, just covered with a light sheet for modesty and warmth. She checked the urinary catheter, the nasogastric tube, the wound drain, the intravenous line—and wondered how Ginny would feel about all the tubes going in and out of his battered body.

Awful, probably. It was a horrible shock, although, as a doctor, of course, she'd have seen it often enough. It must be different when it was your own partner, though. Ryan moved restlessly, and Ronnie shifted one of the pillows a fraction to prop his head better. He relaxed against it, his eyes fluttering shut, and he seemed to drift off again.

Then Ginny came into the room, looking taut as a

bowstring and worried sick, and as if he knew she was there his eyes instantly opened.

'Hi, honey,' he murmured, and Ginny swallowed hard and blinked away tears.

'Hi, yourself. What the hell are you trying to do to me, O'Connor?'

He gave a lopsided grin. 'Who, me? You mean you care?'

She gave up trying to be brave then, and sat down in the big comfy chair beside him, laid her head on the edge of the bed and sobbed. His hand, the one without the drip, came out and rested on her head, and she grabbed it like a lifeline and hung on until she had herself under control again.

Then she lifted her head and glared at him. 'What were you doing? I gather you tried to get the knife off him! You must be mad!'

Nick put a restraining hand on her shoulder. 'Can you tell him off when he's better?' he said with gentle humour. 'I think she's glad you're still alive, Ryan,' he added to their patient, and Ryan's mouth twitched in what could have been a smile.

'He needs to rest, Ginny, and so do you,' Ronnie told her. 'Can I get you a blanket and a pillow, so you can make yourself comfortable beside him?'

Ginny nodded, scrubbing the tears from her cheeks and looking embarrassed. 'I'm sorry. It's just been a hell of a day. I'll be good now.'

Ryan drifted off to sleep again, and for a while Ginny sat and watched the monitors with Ronnie. Then the strain of the day was too much for her, and her eyelids drooped. Ronnie stayed awake and alert, watching, checking, reading the notes and marvelling that he was so well and fit after his ordeal.

At four Ginny woke with a start and sat up. 'Is he all right?' she asked softly, her voice panicky with dread.

'He's fine—nice and steady.'

Ginny sagged back against the chair. 'I thought—I had a dream…' She couldn't finish, but it didn't take much imagination to know what was in the dream.

'Want some tea?' Ronnie asked Ginny.

'Please. I won't sleep again now. Do you want me to make it?'

She shook her head. 'No, it's all right. I'll do it. Holler if he has a problem.'

'I will,' Ginny promised fervently. 'Don't worry.'

Ronnie slipped out of the room and went into the kitchen. A staff nurse followed her in. 'All right?' she asked.

'Yes, he's fine. Can you keep an ear open? I'm just going to report to Mr Sarazin—he's in the duty doctor's room.'

'OK. Will do. If he's about, you couldn't ask him to have a look at Winnie Eddison, could you? She seems to be in a lot of pain—she might have a paralytic ileus.'

'Sure. I'll do it now.'

She left the kettle to boil, and went up the corridor to the duty room and slipped inside. 'Nick?'

'How is he?'

'Fine.' She shut the door and gave herself a moment to adjust to the darkness, then sat on the bed. 'Beth says can you have a look at Mrs Eddison? She thinks she's got a paralytic ileus.'

'Sure.'

She felt his hand curve round her hip and slide up, cupping the back of her neck and drawing her down.

Their lips met in the darkness, tender and regretful. 'I want you,' he murmured.

'Mmm,' she agreed, resting her head against his shoulder. 'Not a good idea. I can't leave Ryan that long and it might cause a bit of a stir amongst the gossips.'

He chuckled and patted her leg. 'Very likely. Go on, then, you temptress. Go back to your patient and let me get up. I'll go and see Mrs Eddison and come and find you. Any chance of a cup of tea?'

'The kettle's on,' she told him, and dropped a kiss on his rough, scratchy jaw. 'You might want to shave before you come out—you feel like a pirate.'

'I thought women found that very sexy,' he murmured in a gravelly voice.

'They do,' she assured him, and stood up before she did something stupid, like tear off her clothes and jump in beside him. 'I'll make your tea. Don't be long.'

She tugged her uniform straight, ran a hand over her hair and went back to the kitchen. The kettle had boiled, so she made three cups of tea, took them into Ryan's room and caught Ginny in tears.

'What's wrong?' she asked urgently, scanning the monitors. Surely nothing had happened in the few minutes she'd been gone?

'Oh, I'm just being silly,' Ginny assured her with a watery, apologetic smile. 'He seems fine. I can't believe it. I thought he was dying.'

'*Everybody* thought he was dying,' Ronnie told her gently. 'I think they just wouldn't let him.'

Ginny nodded. 'You don't always have a choice,' she pointed out. 'No matter how hard you fight, sometimes the injury's just too severe. I know that. I've been there. They say it never happens to you, but this time I really thought it had.'

'Well, he's made it through the surgery, anyway,' Ronnie said guardedly. She didn't want to overdo the optimism, because there was still a long way to go and there was many a slip 'twixt the cup and the lip, and all that. She passed Ginny a mug of tea.

'I woke Nick. He'll be here in a minute. He's going to have a look at one of the other patients, and then come and have his tea.'

Ginny nodded. 'It was kind of him to stay the night here.'

'I think he just didn't want to take any risks—not after spending so long yesterday struggling with leaks. If anything else crops up, he wants to be in reach.'

'He's very kind.'

'I'm sure Ryan would do the same for him.'

'Probably.'

They shared a smile, then Ginny turned her attention back to the monitors. 'We just have to watch and wait now, I suppose,' she said quietly.

Ronnie nodded. In truth there was little else that they could do. Ryan was on a special bed designed for immobile patients so he wouldn't get problems with pressure areas in the few days before he could move again, and in the meantime all Ronnie had to do was keep a constant eye on all his systems and let him rest.

Nick came and had his tea, chatting quietly with Ginny while Ronnie stretched her legs down the corridor and spent a few minutes staring into space.

Nick looked much tidier and more conventional now, she thought absently—clean-shaven, bright-eyed and dressed in clean, pressed clothes, he was a far cry from the exhausted surgeon of last night or the filthy, scruffy and yet sexy man she'd spent the weekend with.

So many people all rolled into one, she mused. Would the real Nicholas Sarazin please stand up?

'Penny for them.'

She jumped, startled by his silent approach, and turned and smiled at him. 'You sneaked up on me,' she chastised softly.

'What are you doing?'

'Just taking five. I was looking at the stars.' And remembering the weekend, she thought to herself. It seemed a lifetime since he'd held her in his arms.

He rested a hand on her shoulder and looked up into the night sky. 'Beautiful, isn't it? There'll be a frost.'

'It was icy last night when I came in.'

She turned and leaned against the wall. 'Is Ryan all right?'

'I've left Ginny in charge for a moment. I thought I might go back to bed—try and catch another couple of hours before morning. Want to wake me at seven with a cup of tea?' His lazy, beguiling smile was her undoing.

'You'll get spoilt,' she warned.

'Mmm. I could learn to enjoy it.'

And I could spend a lifetime doing it, given half a chance, she thought. She pushed herself away from the wall. 'Go on, then, go back to bed and I'll go and watch Ryan. I'll wake you if there's any change.'

He walked back with her, telling her about Mrs Eddison's paralytic ileus, and then paused at the door of the duty room. He seemed almost tempted to ask her in, but that was just wishful thinking. There was no way he would ask, and no way she could go.

She dredged up a smile. 'I'll see you at seven. Sleep tight, you lucky thing.'

'Won't you have tomorrow off?'

'Do you mean today? Probably not. Depends if they can get cover. I'll work till midday in any case. I can't remember who's on this afternoon. If it's Trish, I can hand over to her. If it's Vicky, I shouldn't, really. She's a bit young to have so much responsibility and since she's been engaged she's been a bit elsewhere on the concentration front.'

He chuckled softly. 'Elsewhere—I like that. I know the feeling.'

So did Ronnie, but she wasn't admitting it to him in a lifetime. She left him at the door and went back to Ryan and Ginny.

'How are you?'

'Sore as heck.'

Ronnie smiled and sat down beside Ryan on the comfy chair. 'So use the pump.'

He gave the infusion pump with its ready supply of pain relief a jaundiced glare. 'I have. It's the bone. It just scrapes every time I move—and the physio's just gone.'

'Ah. Torture time.'

'Tell me about it,' he snorted. 'She keeps making me cough.'

'You need to.' Ronnie ran a practised eye over the monitors.

'I'm fine. I'm watching myself. Don't worry, I'll holler if I start to go downhill.'

Ronnie chuckled. 'I doubt if you will now. It's been three days—it's time you got up.'

'Very funny,' he growled.

She rolled her eyes. 'Why is it,' she mused out loud, 'that doctors are so good at dishing it out and so bad at taking it?'

'Because they know how much it's going to hurt?' he offered drily.

'Could be.' She flashed him a smile. 'Nevertheless, I think you could sit out for a while this morning.'

'I quite agree—time we got you back down to A and E and working again, instead of lying about.'

Ronnie threw Nick a grin over her shoulder. 'Hi, there. Come and help me bully him. He doesn't want to get up.'

'Oh, he wants to get up,' Ryan corrected her. 'He just doesn't want to hurt like the blazes while he does it!'

'I'll let you get over your physio, then we'll help you out. Have another squirt from the pump in the meantime, help it wear off.'

'I've squeezed the thing dry. It won't deliver.'

'So yell when you've had the next dose.'

He gave a careful snort of disgust.

'Promise,' Ronnie threatened gently.

'I promise,' he sighed, and dropped his head back. He looked better, she thought, but not much. She supposed he'd come about as close to death as one would wish to, and not unnaturally it showed. However, thanks to Nick and his team, it looked as though all the injuries had been found and dealt with, so it was just simply a question of sitting out the healing time.

Not easy, when you were a busy, active man with a restless mind and a hatred of being dependent—and Ryan hated it.

Nick examined his handiwork, praised himself for his brilliance and followed Ronnie out, grinning. 'Don't you think I'm stunning?' he said with a chuckle.

'I don't need to—you're already sufficiently vain without my help. Come on, you've got a ward full of pre-ops to reassure and check over, and some post-ops, needing your attention.'

'How's Mrs Eddison's paralytic ileus?'

'Better.'

'Good.' He paused, well away from any ears that might be listening to their conversation. 'What are you doing tonight?'

'Nothing. Why?'

'The electricians have finished the rewiring and the plumber's making progress—I thought we could have a look at the house. Maybe pick up a take-away and eat it there by the fire.'

The message in his eyes was unmistakable, and Ronnie was tempted—too tempted to refuse. She smiled. 'Sounds good. What time?'

'Meet me there at seven?' he suggested.

'OK.'

'Good.' His eyes tracked over her, then returned to her face. 'Let's go and see these patients before I forget I'm supposed to be behaving and drag you into the linen cupboard.'

The evening was frustrating. The house was a mess from end to end, of course, but progress had certainly been made. There was no drawing-room floor to have a picnic on, though, because the boards were up, and the other rooms were at the front of the house or else it wasn't possible to have a fire in them—and it was too darned cold without one for what they had in mind!

In the end they sat in the bottom tower room with its newly reglazed window and panoramic view of the street, and ate their Chinese take-away in front of a properly drawing fire and with a safe foot of space between them.

Frustrating, but possibly a good idea, Ronnie reluctantly acknowledged—and it didn't stop Nick from spreading out a blanket on the floor under the window-seat and lying down with her and kissing her senseless, which was even more frustrating but probably very good for their self-control.

Of course, if they hadn't had to be so obsessive about keeping it all a secret, then they could have been in her bed or his, doing what their bodies and minds craved to do, without any feelings of guilt or shame.

Ronnie slept badly that night, with Nick just on the other side of the wall, and in the morning it was hard to find a smile at work.

'What's wrong?' Ryan asked softly as she tended to his drip.

'Nothing,' she said, pulling out the cannula and taping the little hole in his arm. 'Press that for me.'

Obediently he put a finger over the plaster and pressed. 'Funny-looking nothing. Is it Nick?'

Her head snapped up. 'What about him?'

Ryan shrugged, then winced. 'Just a thought. He was all over you like a rash at the ball. You couldn't have fitted a credit card between you, you were so close.'

She felt herself colour. 'You're imagining it.'

'And am I imagining the looks he gives you? Or the look you get when he's around? Come on, Ronnie. I know how it is. I've been married twice, head over heels in love both times. I can recognise the symptoms.'

'You should be resting,' she told him stiffly, avoiding his eye.

His hand caught her wrist, and she couldn't pull away for fear of hurting him. 'Look at me,' he ordered.

'No.'

'Yes. Ronnie, you can talk to me. It won't go any further. Sometimes it helps to have a shoulder to lean on.'

She gulped, blinking back the sudden tears that took her by surprise, and sank down onto the chair.

'That's better. Now, tell Uncle Ry all about it.'

She sniffed and gave him a watery grin. 'Oh, Ryan, there's nothing to tell. We're having an affair, but he's got kids—his wife died four years ago.'

'Sounds all very familiar to me,' Ryan said gently. 'Don't tell me—he's worried about hurting the kids and he's keeping you a deep, dark secret.'

Ronnie's head snapped up. 'How did you know?'

He gave a wry laugh. 'Been there, done that, worn out the T-shirt. Ginny had a word for it—she used to say she was Category Three. Not wife, not colleague, but sex slave. I thought she was mad, but afterwards I realised just how much it had hurt her. I never meant to, Ronnie, just as I'm sure Nick doesn't mean to hurt you, but at least you're an adult and you've got choices. The children in these relationships have no choices.'

'No. I know that. I'm just being self-pitying and behaving like a spoilt brat.'

He reached out his hand and patted her fist, clenched round a handful of blanket on the edge of the bed. 'No. You're in love, and you want to shout it from the rooftops, and you can't. If it helps, he probably feels the same.'

Ronnie hadn't thought of that. Not that it changed anything, of course, but maybe it would help her to be more accepting of the situation. She nodded. 'Thanks, Ryan—and, please, don't say anything to Nick. He'd hate it if he knew I'd talked about us.'

Ryan smiled tiredly. 'Don't worry, I won't.' His eyes slipped shut, and she straightened his bedclothes and left him to sleep. He was still very weak and needed time to heal.

She wondered how much time Nick would take before he was healed enough to love again—if at all.

Patience wasn't her strong suit.

'So, what's this I hear about you sneaking out of Nick's house after the ball?' Meg said, leaning forward and scanning Ronnie's face eagerly.

'Oh, Meg, how did you hear about that?' she wailed, blushing furiously and burying her face in her mug.

'Sam's mother told me. She was looking out for him because she knew he hadn't come home, and she saw you through the window, just as he got back.'

Ronnie groaned. 'Hell. And I thought no one knew!'

Meg laughed. 'You can't do anything in this town without people finding out, far less this road! So, tell me all about it!' she continued, leaning forward again with that eager look still on her face. 'That new dress obviously did the trick.'

Ronnie sighed. 'There's nothing much to tell, really. We went to the ball, came back and I stayed the night with him.'

'And since?'

She thought of the weekend of decorating, and the frustration of the previous night, and closed her eyes. 'It's...difficult.'

'Because of the kids,' Meg said, understanding without having to have it spelled out. 'But they're on half-term at the moment—they're away. Why aren't you round there all night, taking advantage of that gorgeous man—or are you shinnying over the fence, you sly thing?'

Ronnie shook her head. 'Unfortunately not,' she said wryly.

'You need your bumps felt,' Meg snorted, getting up and putting the kettle on again. 'If a man like that showed the slightest interest in me, I'd be in there like a shot.'

'That's the trouble, of course,' Ronnie said softly. 'He only does show the slightest interest. Oh, he's keen enough if we get a chance, but he's obsessive about the kids finding out.'

'But surely they will?' Meg said. 'Children aren't stupid. They'll notice, no matter how careful you are.'

'That's why I said there's nothing going on. There really isn't, and I don't think there ever will be, unfortunately.'

'So no wedding bells?' Meg said sympathetically.

Ronnie sighed. 'No. No wedding bells—not as long as he's got the children, anyway. While they're around there's no danger of us getting married—not even close.' There was a thud, and the front door slammed back against the hall wall. Meg lifted her head. 'Jimmy?' she said, and he appeared in the doorway. 'Hello, love. Had fun?' she asked.

He nodded. 'I've been playing football with Mickey,' he said. 'Hi, Ronnie. What's for supper, Mum?'

'Shepherd's pie. You staying, Ronnie?'

She shook her head. 'I must go,' she said. 'I'll raid the freezer and then do my ironing. I'll see you. Thanks for the coffee.'

'My pleasure. Keep me posted.'

Ronnie went home, closed her front door and leaned

against it with a sigh. Nick was away for the weekend, and she wouldn't see him again until Sunday night when he came back with the children.

Funny, she'd never really felt lonely until they'd moved in. She'd been tempted to have supper with Meg, but that was silly. She had to deal with this. After all, it seemed very likely she was going to be alone for a long, long time, because Nick Sarazin and his children were going to be a hard act to follow.

She decided to go and visit her father and stepmother for the weekend. Perhaps that would take her mind off him—and she wouldn't have to deal with her ironing!

CHAPTER EIGHT

'GOOD weekend?'

'Sort of. I've been to Southampton to see my father.'
Ronnie perched on the edge of Ryan's bed and checked
his pulse.

'So that's why Nick's looking grumpy,' Ryan
mused.

'Nonsense. Shut up, I'm counting.'

Ryan grinned and she ignored him, losing count yet
again and having to start from scratch for the third
time. 'You're a nuisance—but you'll live. That's nice
and steady. How are you feeling?'

'Better than I was, but still a long way off.'

'I'm sure.' She eyed his colour thoughtfully. 'You
don't look anaemic.'

'I can't be. They pumped gallons of blood into me,
by all accounts.'

'And you promptly squandered it. You, of all people,
should know better,' she teased, and stood up. 'Time
to sit out?'

He groaned, but obediently swung his legs over the
side of the bed and sat himself up. 'Ow, ow-ow-ow,'
he muttered under his breath.

'Coward.'

'Yeah, right. Just give me a hand and shut up.'

She helped him into the chair, settled him down and
tucked a blanket round his knees. 'I feel about a hundred,' he grumbled. 'All I need is a nightcap on my
head—you know, one of those pointy ones with a little
bobble on the end?'

She chuckled and left him to it, wading through a stack of professional journals he hadn't had time to read. She'd take him for a walk later, and maybe get one of the porters to take him down to A and E to see his friends. Ginny came in when she could with the children, but they couldn't spend all day with him and he was feeling a little isolated.

Not for long. She was halfway down the corridor with him in a very sedate and steady walk when a crowd of doctors and nurses came round the corner and cheered.

'Hey, it's the boss!' one of them yelled, and his face cracked into a grin.

'Hello, guys and girls,' he said with a laugh. 'Come to brighten up my life?'

'We've brought you a present—us.'

'How are you?'

'You don't look too bad—isn't it time you were back?'

'Yeah, we miss you. Nobody to nag us.'

Ronnie waved at them all to quieten them down, and then carefully helped Ryan back to bed. 'Now, not too much noise, you lot, or I'll throw you out—savvy? I can't have you disturbing my post-ops.'

'Yes, ma'am!' one of them said, and she recognised Matt Jordan, the other Canadian A and E consultant.

'You—keep them in order,' she told him firmly, and he grinned and winked.

'I'll do my best.'

It wasn't good enough. After half an hour of steadily escalating racket, she went back into the room and good-naturedly threw them all out. Ryan had had enough anyway, she could tell, and he was only being polite.

She shut the door behind them and turned to him.
'You OK?'

'Yes—I will be. I think I could use some sleep.'

She laughed softly. 'I expect so. That lot are enough
to try anyone's patience.'

'I can forgive them—they saved my life,' he reminded her, and she smiled and tucked the bedclothes
round him.

'So they did. You rest now. I expect Ginny will be
in later, won't she?'

He nodded tiredly, and she left him to it. He would
probably sleep for ages, and it would do him good. For
most of the first week he hadn't been able to sleep very
well because of the pain and the unnatural position.
Now at least he could lie down. She closed the door
softly behind her, and went to check that Oliver
Henderson's post-ops were all stable and comfortable.

'So will you be done by Thursday?'

The plumber scratched his jaw and stared into space,
while Nick hung onto his temper with difficulty. 'Probably,' he replied at last.

'Is that very probably, or probably not?'

The man grinned. 'Depends.'

'On?'

He heaved a sigh. 'Well, that water tank in the loft,
for one. And, of course, if the pipes in the bathroom
all have to be concealed, then I've got to box them in
on the wall behind—that's going to take longer.'

Nick nodded. 'But could you be out of the rest of
the house by then so the decorators can start? I just
want the hall and drawing room clear initially, and the
kids' bedrooms, so we can slap on a quick coat of paint
and tart it up to start with.'

'Hmm. Pushing it.'

'But?'

'Reckon we might manage that,' the plumber conceded.

Nick felt he'd gone ten rounds with a world heavyweight, but he had agreement—albeit reluctant—that he could bring the decorators in to start at the end of the week, and for now that would have to do.

He looked around the house in tired disbelief. So much to do. Just looking at it made him feel exhausted. If only he could afford to have it all done by someone else. Well, he probably could, but only by dipping into Anna's life assurance, and he'd got that invested for the children.

He leaned on the doorpost in the drawing room and looked at the floor in front of the fireplace where he and Ronnie had made love that weekend. It seemed ages ago. Too long.

He glanced at his watch, and sighed. He had to go home and fetch the children from Meg, then fight with them about homework and bathing and bedtime.

And then, once they were in bed, there was nothing to do but sit and think about Ronnie, about the softness of her skin, and the warmth of her smile, and the feel of her arms around him—

He shoved himself away from the doorframe with a growl of frustration, and headed for the door. 'I'm off, Steve,' he called to the plumber.

There was a grunt from under the kitchen sink, and he let himself out of the front door. He should be feeling good about the progress the house was making and the way the kids were settling down.

Instead, he wanted more.

He wanted Ronnie, and he couldn't have her.

He slammed the car door, gunned it out of the drive into the traffic and vented his spleen on the throttle.

*   *   *

'Are you sure it means that?'

Ben screwed up his nose thoughtfully, and Ronnie sat back and waited for him to see what he was doing wrong.

'Oh—you have to take it away,' he said eventually, and Ronnie tousled his hair and grinned.

'Well done. Right, Amy, let's hear this reading, then.'

They were settled down at the kitchen table, poring over Amy's reading book, when Nick rang the doorbell.

'I'll get it,' Ben yelled, and ran to the door.

'Hi—I thought I'd lost you,' Nick said, and his deep, gravelly voice did funny things to Ronnie's insides. She forced herself to stay there and not rush to greet him with the same enthusiasm as Ben.

She couldn't stop herself from returning his smile when he came into the kitchen, though. 'Hi,' she said softly. 'Meg had a headache—I hope you don't mind them coming here.'

'No, of course not,' he said, and settled his hips against the worktop just opposite her, brightening up her view no end. 'I hope you didn't mind.'

'Absolutely not. Coffee or tea?' she asked. 'Or wine? There might be some red in the cupboard.'

'Wine sounds wonderful,' he said wearily and, turning a chair round, he straddled it, looking sexier than he had any right to. She busied herself with the corkscrew, and then set the glass down in front of him on the edge of the table.

He smiled gratefully up at her and raised the glass, and the message in his eyes was unmistakable. She felt a terrible urge to laugh—or cry. She wasn't sure which, but there was a real feel to the situation of, 'Hi, honey, I'm home.' Any minute now she would start asking him about his day—which was absurd, because she knew all about his day. She'd been there.

Oh, knickers, she thought tiredly.

Amy was still reading out loud, her blunt little finger following the words, hesitating every now and again, and Nick was prompting her when necessary.

He was good, she thought. He didn't just tell her the answer, he helped her to work the word out, and it was obvious he'd done it hundreds of times before.

Without her.

She picked up her glass and sipped from it, and let him deal with the children. It was his job. They were his children, and they weren't ever going to be hers.

Even if she did occasionally let herself pretend they would.

'The decorators go in on Thursday,' Nick volunteered, swivelling round to see her better. '*If* the plumber's out of the way. He's being very cagey about it, and I don't know if he's just being awkward or if he really is behind.'

'Let's hope he's just being awkward. Do you owe him money?'

Nick nodded.

'Good. He's more likely to do the work if he stands to get a nice fat chunk of dosh when it's finished. Human nature, isn't it? We all need a reward, and sometimes just doing the job well isn't enough.'

She reached over and topped up his wine, and he gave her a tired smile. 'Don't give me too much—I've got to cook for this lot yet.'

'We could have pizza,' Amy suggested absently without lifting her head. 'I like chicken and sweetcorn.'

Ben and Nick turned to stare at her, but she kept her head bent over her book, her little finger moving slowly across the page, her lips silently forming the words.

Nick looked up and sought Ronnie's eyes. 'Pizza?' he said incredulously.

She shrugged and suppressed a smile. 'Apparently.'

'Fancy pizza?' he asked her.

'It's up to you. It's your supper.'

'Join us,' he said, and there was a plea in his voice she couldn't ignore. Not that she tried.

'That would be lovely,' she told him. 'Your place or mine?'

'Mine. We can put the children in the bath while we finish the bottle that way.'

Was he thawing?

Or just as desperate for her company as she was for his?

Or, in the end, would that add up to the same thing?

The pizza arrived just as they were settling down in front of the gas fire in Nick's sitting room. Ronnie had hardly spent any time there, and it seemed strange. A mirror image of her own, and furnished by the hospital in almost identical style to hers, it was bare and bleak and characterless, like a waiting room.

Like hers had been when she'd moved in, but she'd lived there for years now and had made it her own. He'd only been there five weeks or so, and for them it was very temporary. He had an excuse.

They sat round in a ring, with the pizza boxes open on the coffee-table, and pulled slices off at random, ignoring niceties like plates and cutlery. Amy's first slice had a great dangling string of cheese hanging off it, and it trailed down her chin and gave her and Ben the giggles.

It was impossible not to join in their silliness, and over their heads she caught sight of Nick's face. He looked years younger, truly happy, and she wondered if she was a part of that happiness, or still on the outside, looking in.

He leaned across the table and wiped Amy's chin gently with a tissue. 'Mucky urchin,' he said affectionately, and Ronnie felt even more isolated.

Then he looked up and caught her eye, and winked, and she felt all her worries dissolve. Give him time, she told herself. Do what Ryan said and give him time.

She settled back with her glass of wine, and watched them clean up the last few slices of pizza in no time flat. Then Nick went out to the kitchen and came back with bowls heaped with ice cream, bananas and chocolate sauce, and then, while Ronnie cleared up the mess and made coffee, Nick hustled the children through the bathtime routine and into bed.

'I'll come up in twenty minutes to put your lights out,' he called as he came down, and Ronnie looked up as he walked into the kitchen.

'Coffee,' she said, holding out his mug, and he took it, smiling gratefully.

'Lifesaver,' he murmured. 'Come and sit down.'

They sat at each end of the sofa, their hands meshed on the centre cushion, and then Ronnie turned and swung her legs up so her toes were tucked under his thigh and she could feel the warmth of his leg against her feet.

His hand came down and snuggled her ankles, and she settled her head against the back of the settee and thought that life couldn't really get much better. 'What are you doing at the weekend?' he asked drowsily, breaking the long, companionable silence.

'Working Saturday, nothing Sunday. Why?'

He gave a slow, wry smile. 'Because we're decorating the kids' bedrooms. I wondered if you wanted to help.'

She chuckled. 'I expect I might be coerced into it,' she agreed. 'Any idea what you're doing?'

'Well, Amy predictably wants yellow again, but most of her bedding is yellow, so that's fine. Ben said something about spaceships and planets, but I don't know what we can do about that.'

Ronnie sat up a little more and shuffled her bottom back against the arm of the sofa. 'How about a very dark blue ceiling?' she suggested, seeing it in her mind's eye. 'With stars and planets on it. You can get maps. My sister did it for her son a couple of years ago—she might still have the map. You have the light fitting for the sun, and work out from there.'

'On dark blue?' he said sceptically.

'Yes—almost black. You hardly notice it, it's like a stage, going up into the bit where they hang the lights and hoist up the scenery—you know.'

'Or the night sky, even.'

She laughed at the dry tone in his voice. 'Even that,' she agreed with a smile. 'And then you graduate the colour down so that by eye level it's soft grey-blue, and by the skirting board it's white. You can stencil spaceships and satellites and things in silver around the top, and it's wonderful.'

'It sounds it. Can you ask your sister about the map?'

'Sure—and now I'm going to go home and do my ironing and get an early night, because I have to be at work for seven tomorrow and you need to go and turn their lights out.'

He stood up and pulled her to her feet but, instead of releasing her, he drew her into his arms. 'I wish you could stay. I wish we could spend the night together.'

'Maybe another time,' she suggested.

'Maybe next weekend—not this one, but the one after. We'll go to a hotel—I'll treat you. We'll have a lazy, romantic dinner, and a lie-in in the morning.'

She swallowed hard. 'That sounds wonderful,' she said breathlessly.

'Good.' He lowered his head and brushed her lips with his. 'Now, go home before I do something silly and irresponsible.'

It sounded tempting, but she stepped back and made herself walk towards the door. 'I'll see you tomorrow. Thanks for the pizza.'

'My pleasure. Thanks for the wine.'

He kissed her again, right inside the front door, where the children could easily have seen them if they'd come to the head of the stairs, and then he opened the door and she went out into the chilly night, and back into her own house.

It seemed incredibly quiet and empty.

Ryan made great strides that week. Perhaps because he could sleep properly at last, he seemed to find his natural reserves and bounced back. By Thursday he was wandering around the ward, sticking his nose in everyone's notes and getting in the way.

'Do you think you should be at home?' Ronnie suggested with a smile as he gatecrashed her, giving report.

He smiled and propped himself up against the wall. 'Good heavens, no. I'd have nobody to irritate and nothing to do. I'd go crazy.'

'Well, we aren't having you in here, driving us nuts, for the next four weeks until you're fit to go back to work, so perhaps you'd better send Ginny out to buy you some jigsaws or something.'

He snorted and eased himself carefully away from the wall. 'I can tell when I'm not wanted,' he grumbled good-naturedly, and ambled off up the ward, stopping to chat to the patients on the way.

'He's going to find it very hard convalescing,' Ronnie mused, watching him.

'He'll cope. He'll have to. He's nothing like fit enough to go back to work yet,' Vicky said pragmatically. 'He'll just have to learn to amuse himself. Buy a computer game or something.'

'Or read that stack of journals. That should keep him quiet.'

They laughed and moved on to the next patient, but Ronnie kept her eye on Ryan. He went into the day room, and she made a mental note to go and see him in a while. Perhaps he needed someone from Occupational Therapy to give him something to do.

Andy Graham, Nick's first patient, came in to visit them later. He'd been transferred to Orthopaedics because one of his legs hadn't lined up well and he had to have a series of operations, and he went into the day room and found Ryan, who had been on duty when he'd come in to A and E.

Ronnie found them playing cards, both of them cheating outrageously, and she left them to it. It kept Ryan out of her hair, and Andy wasn't doing any harm and was obviously bored to death with his slow recovery.

She rang the ward to let them know where he was, and over the next few days it became a routine. It seemed to keep Ryan sane, which was just as well because he periodically spiked a temperature, and Nick was unhappy to let him go home until he was truly well again.

On Sunday morning Ronnie was looking forward to her first day off in ages. She woke up to the sound of

Nick and the children chatting in his bedroom at some ghastly hour. She couldn't hear the words, but she could understand the tone of voice.

The children wanted to go and decorate, and Nick wanted to sleep. Judging by Nick's howls of outrage and the giggles from the children, they were winning. She turned over, snuggled down again and smiled. She'd get up later—much later—and go and help them…

'I don't know why you think we needed such an early start anyway,' she grumbled, perched at the top of a stepladder slapping midnight blue paint on Ben's ceiling.

'Perhaps by the time you get down to the skirting boards, you will,' Nick said with a grin. He was painting the walls white so that she could bring the graduated colour down over them in a wash, and it would have been so easy to reach over with the roller and splat him with navy paint.

She debated it, and gave up. He was right. There was a lot to do, and Amy was grumbling that she just had plain yellow walls and she needed something pretty.

'I could do a stencil round Amy's walls,' Ronnie suggested. 'Clowns and balloons and little animals, or something. Perhaps a circus frieze?'

'She's got sort of circus striped bedding,' Nick mumbled from the corner. 'That would look nice.'

'Do we need to see the bedding to choose the colours?' Ronnie asked, reaching for the last bit of white.

'No, I've done it the same colour as the last room, to make it easier.'

He straightened up, his hands on the small of his

back, and stretched. 'I'm getting too old for this,' he grumbled.

Ronnie laughed unsympathetically. 'Not enough exercise, that's your trouble.'

'No opportunity,' he said, looking up at her on the ladder with an unmistakably suggestive smile. 'Next weekend, however...'

She grinned and climbed down the ladder, brushing against him tantalisingly. 'Mmm. Lovely thought. Exercise has never been more appealing!'

'Have you done it?'

They looked round at Ben, who was standing in the doorway, looking puzzled. 'We're getting there, sprog,' Nick said affectionately. 'What do you think so far?' He peered around, his face a little crestfallen. 'I thought my walls were going to be sort of shady,' he said, and his voice was rich with disappointment.

'They are,' Ronnie assured him. 'We've just got to wait for the white to dry and we can start painting them. We're going to look at Amy's now while we wait.'

She put her roller in a plastic bag and wiped her hands on her old shirt. No matter how careful she was, she got paint all over herself always. There was probably some in her hair, and she knew for a fact there was a smear of it on her nose.

Ah, well.

She followed Nick next door into Amy's room, and cannoned into his back in the doorway.

'Oh, Amy,' he said disbelievingly, and Ronnie peered round his arm and gasped.

Amy, obviously having decided that Ben was having too much attention, had decided to paint flowers on her bedroom walls. Huge, blue and white flowers that splodged and dribbled down the walls, and had obviously splodged and dribbled down Amy as well. Paint was in her hair, all over her clothes, and after one look at her father's face she dissolved into tears and dropped the brush on her shoes.

Nick closed his eyes, leaned against the wall and counted softly under his breath.

When he was in the mid-twenties, Ronnie elbowed him out of the way and took over.

'Whoops,' she said gently, and picked the brush up off Amy's newish trainers. 'I think we need to get you and your clothes into the bath, sweetheart, while Daddy sorts out your walls. We were just talking about some circusy things—animals and balloons and clowns and big tops and so forth—does that sound nice?'

'I want flowers,' she hiccuped, and started to wail again.

'We'll discuss it. Let's get you cleaned up first. Nick, do we have hot water—Nick?' she added, a little more sharply, and he opened his eyes and scanned the room again, before focusing on her.

'What?' he croaked. If ever there was a desperate man, she thought with an inward smile.

'Hot water?'

'Oh. Um—yes, should be. Use their bathroom—the bath still needs to be restored, so she won't be able to do it any damage. Unlike the walls in here...'

'How about a nice wash over with a sponge and a bucket before it dries, and then another coat of yellow, hmm?' she coaxed, and ushered Amy into the bathroom before he killed her.

Half an hour later the miserable little miscreant was at least substantially paint-free, and so were her clothes and trainers. Everything, child included, was soggy, but there didn't seem to be any towels.

Ronnie pulled the lever that lifted the huge brass

plug out of the bath, and told Amy not to move while she found something to dry her with.

'I've got a stack of old towels for washing down the walls and things—in the kitchen in a carrier bag,' Nick told her, swiping, grim-lipped, at the tenacious flowers.

Whoops. Ronnie ran down to the kitchen, found the towels and ran back up to Amy, who hadn't moved so much as a hair. She scooped the little girl out of the bath, towelled her off and wrapped her in another one, then rubbed her hair as dry as she could.

'I don't know what you're going to wear, poppet,' she said thoughtfully. 'What about if I give you my jumper?'

She dressed Amy in her own socks and underwear, and pulled the jumper over the child's head, turning up the sleeves about six times so that the slightly blue little hands could peek out of the cuffs.

'I think you've got something to say to Daddy, don't you?' she said gently, and Amy nodded and clung to her leg.

'I wanted flowers,' she said, and started to cry again. 'Ben's having spaceships.'

'I know.' She hunkered down on the floor at Amy's level and looked her in the eye. 'Do you want flowers, or circus things?'

'Circus,' Amy said. 'With flowers,' she added as an afterthought.

'Circus with flowers,' Ronnie said in confirmation. 'Let's go and see what Daddy says.'

Daddy was putty in her hands, of course. He sighed, shook his head and held out his arms, and Amy rushed into them and buried her head in his shoulder. He straightened up, her little legs wrapped round his waist, and hugged her while she cried.

Ronnie left them to it. He was quite capable of dealing with his own six-year-old daughter, and if she was off the scene too long, Ben might start on his room and then all hell would break loose!

It took several evenings and a few more tins of paint, but by the following Thursday the children's rooms were finished except for new curtains, and they were ready to move in.

The carpet for the hall, stairs and landing, the snug and the children's rooms came on Friday, and on Saturday Nick delivered the children to their grandparents and came back.

It was the weekend of their planned getaway, and Ronnie was feeling almost sick with nerves.

'I wish you'd tell me where we were going,' she said plaintively.

He tapped the side of his nose. 'Secret,' he told her. 'I have to go over to the house for a while and talk to the plumber and the decorator—why don't you meet me there at three?'

'What should I pack?' she asked. 'How smart is it?'

He shrugged. 'It's an old inn in the middle of nowhere—just a dressy pub, really. It has a wonderful reputation for being a romantic getaway.'

'Says who?'

'The brochure. I picked it up from the tourist information office.'

She smiled. 'Dressy pub. Right. Thanks. I'll see you later.'

She spent the day pampering herself—and, goodness knows, she needed it. She'd spent all week stencilling walls and drawing clowns, and her nails were a mess, her hair was full of paint and she felt generally scruffy.

She dressed in smart trousers, ankle boots and a fine

silk blouse, and just hoped that it would be dressy enough for his 'dressy pub'.

She arrived at the house at ten to three, and found Nick on his mobile phone in the newly completed hall. He beckoned her in, finished the call and drew her into his arms. 'You look lovely—mmm, and you smell wonderful.'

'Clean, you mean!' she said with a chuckle, and looked around. 'This house is beginning to look really good. I love the carpet.'

'It's worked, hasn't it? I'm delighted. Thank you for helping me find the house. In fact, thank you for all sorts of things. Let's go and celebrate.'

He ushered her out, parked her car on the drive instead of his and shut the high gates behind it so nobody would know it was there. Secrets, again, she thought heavily. Oh, well. She didn't really want it publicised that she was going off for a dirty weekend with him. Sometimes secrecy was just another word for privacy, and they were very short on that.

The hotel was about an hour away, down pretty twisting lanes, past hedges just breaking into leaf, and when they arrived the daffodils along the drive were just beginning to open.

'Oh, it's pretty,' she said as the pub came into view. It was thatched, and the stableyard behind had been converted to form part of the accommodation. Tubs of bulbs and polyanthus brought touches of colour to the courtyard area, and more were clustered round the door.

They parked the car and took their luggage in, and were greeted by a young man behind the desk, who signed them in.

'Up the stairs, turn left and go to the end. It's the last room on the right. Dinner's served from seven till nine, and we serve afternoon tea in the lounge bar until six.

There's also tea- and coffee-making facilities in your room for your convenience. Enjoy your stay.'

'Thank you,' Nick murmured, and took Ronnie's elbow. His hand seemed to tremble slightly, and Ronnie wondered if he was as nervous as she was, or if it was just anticipation.

They found the room easily, and it took a matter of seconds to explore it. Then there didn't seem to be anything left to do to stall.

Ronnie's mouth seemed suddenly dry, and her heart seemed to be hammering in her throat. It was ages since he'd held her—three weeks since that weekend they'd spent working on the house and making love in the intervals.

A man was crossing the courtyard below them, and she watched him and wondered what she was expected to do.

'Ronnie?'

She turned and looked at Nick.

'I don't bite,' he told her gently, and with a little cry she went into his arms...

CHAPTER NINE

'MORNING.'

Ronnie opened her eyes and found Nick there, a playful smile on his lips. He was propped up on one elbow, looking down at her, and she wondered briefly how dishevelled and morning-after-ish she looked.

But only briefly, because, however she looked, it was obvious that Nick was happy with what he saw.

She reached up a hand and rubbed her palm over his cheek. It rasped on the stubble, and she smiled lazily. He looked like a pirate, sexy and forbidden, and she didn't want to move.

Ever.

Her stomach, though, thought otherwise. It growled loudly, and Nick chuckled. 'Was that you or me?'

'Me,' she confessed. 'I'm starving. I must have worked off all that wonderful meal we had last night.'

'Mmm. Me, too. Shall we have breakfast sent up?'

She stretched contentedly. 'How decadent,' she said with a smile.

'Was that a yes?'

'Mmm. Cereal and fruit juice and tea—and toast and marmalade.'

'Not a cooked breakfast?'

She pulled a face. Somehow the thought of all that greasy food curdled her stomach. 'No, not a cooked breakfast.'

'Mind if I do?'

She shook her head. 'Of course not.'

She slipped into the bathroom and showered quickly

while he phoned room service, and was just stepping out of the shower when he came in.

'It's all yours,' she told him, went up on tiptoe to press a kiss on his cheek and left him to it.

He came out minutes later, showered but not shaved, and sat on the edge of the bed. 'You look gorgeous,' he told her softly. 'Good enough to eat. I don't know why I ordered breakfast, I'd rather have you.'

'You haven't shaved,' she said, rubbing her hand over his cheek again.

'No. Do you want me to?'

She shook her head. 'I love your stubble. Very sexy. Shave later.'

He smiled, a lazy, predatory smile and, leaning closer, he lowered his mouth to hers. It was a gentle kiss at first, slow and indolent, without haste. He eased her dressing-gown open and slid a hand inside, cupping her breast, then lowered his head and took the nipple in his mouth.

So much sensation! The heat of his mouth, the firm flick of his tongue, the slight scrape of his beard against her delicate skin. She moaned softly and he shifted her, sliding her down the bed and coming down beside her so she was in his arms again.

'How can I want you again?' he groaned, trailing hot, open-mouthed kisses over her shoulders. 'You're just irresistible—delicious. Mmm.' His lips closed over her other nipple, drawing it deep into his mouth, and she arched against him and cried out softly.

'Easy, sweetheart, easy,' he murmured, and ran his hand over her hip. 'We've got time—'

The sharp tap made them jump. 'Room service— breakfast.'

He jackknifed away from her. 'Um—can you leave it outside, please?' he called, and they heard the clatter of the tray and the retreating footsteps on the carpeted landing.

She started to giggle, and after a second he joined in, falling back onto the bed beside her and pulling her into his arms and hugging her.

'Oh, dear, I thought he was coming in,' he said with a chuckle after a moment.

'Me, too. Is the door locked?'

'Yes—I locked it last night. Don't worry. Now, where were we?'

She slid her hand inside his dressing-gown and down over his hip. 'Ah, yes,' he murmured, and his lips found hers again. Within moments they were swept away again, lost in their own world—so lost that it was a few seconds before they registered the ringing of his mobile phone.

He said something that, if Ben had understood it, would have cost him dearly in the swear-box, and swung his legs over the side of the bed. 'If it's that damn plumber, I'm sacking him,' he growled, fumbling for the phone on the bedside table and finally switching it on.

'Sarazin,' he snapped, and then his voice mellowed. 'Clare—hi. No, sorry, I couldn't find it for a second. How are things? Oh, Lord. Is he all right?'

Ronnie slid up the bed, dragging the covers with her, and watched his face anxiously. 'What is it?' she asked when he'd put the phone down.

'Ben—he's fallen out of a tree and sprained his wrist. Well, they think it's sprained, but it might be broken. Clare's just going to take him to Casualty, but she wants me to meet her there.'

'Where are they going?'

'Addenbrookes. They live just outside Cambridge.'

He glanced at his watch. 'You'll have to come with me. I haven't got time to take you home.'

'You could put me on a train in Cambridge on your way,' she offered, but after a second he shook his head.

'No. Come. Clare needs to get back to Sunday school, and you could sit with Amy. We can be there in half an hour.'

'OK.' She slipped out of bed, put on fresh underwear and the clothes she'd had on last night, and packed her bag. She didn't bother with make-up—Nick seemed in a hurry to get to Ben, and she could understand that. She was in a hurry herself.

'Got everything?' he asked, and she nodded.

'Right.'

He pulled open the door, strode out—and fell headlong over the breakfast tray.

It was too much for Ronnie. She propped herself up in the doorway, covered her mouth with her hand and howled with laughter.

'What happened to your trousers, Daddy?'

Nick gave Amy a jaundiced glower. 'I tripped over my breakfast. I'd put it on the floor.'

'That was silly. Why didn't you change?'

Because he didn't have any other trousers with him—that was the simple answer, but not, of course, one he could give his daughter. Ronnie wondered what he'd say, but he got out of it easily.

'I didn't realise they were so splashed,' he lied, and his look dared Ronnie to disagree with him. She simply arched a brow slightly and looked away, biting the inside of her lip so she didn't laugh again.

It hadn't really been funny. Doors had opened and people had shushed them furiously. One couple had threatened to complain, and as they'd checked out and offered to pay for cleaning up the mess, the receptionist had explained that they'd thought he'd been an employee and he'd dropped a tray.

'We didn't know what they were talking about,' she'd said with a smile. 'Please, don't worry. I'm just glad you weren't hurt.'

Only his pride, Ronnie thought, and suppressed another smile. What a disastrous morning! And then they'd had Clare to deal with, although she'd been so relieved to see them that Ronnie didn't think she would have cared if they'd turned up stark naked!

Later, however, was another matter. They went back to the house, with Ben's sprain confirmed and his support bandage duly signed by the nurse, just as Clare and Peter were coming back from church.

'We don't have a cover story worked out,' Ronnie said out of the side of her mouth.

'Forget it. We'll say we were at the house. Hi. No fracture, just a sprain,' he said to his in-laws, and then took Ronnie's elbow and ushered her forward. 'Clare, Peter, this is Veronica Matthews, my next-door neighbour and surgical ward sister. Ronnie, you've met Clare, of course, and this is Peter.'

Ronnie, her heart pounding like that of a cornered criminal, dredged up what she hoped was a normal smile and shook their hands. 'Hello. Nice to meet you.'

'You got here very quickly—you must have been over this way,' Peter said to Nick, inadvertently wandering into the middle of a minefield.

'Um—we were hoping to look at an architectural salvage firm,' he lied.

'Oh, really? I didn't know they were open on Sundays.'

'Ah. I don't know. We were just going to try and find it,' he ad-libbed, digging a bigger hole.

'You didn't shave,' Ben said, eyeing him curiously. 'You *always* shave.'

'I forgot,' he said, and changed the subject firmly back to Ben's arm.

Nevertheless, Ronnie felt their eyes on her, their curiosity thinly veiled, and hoped to high heaven that she wouldn't turn scarlet and give the game away. She was, however, growing more and more conscious of the little patch of whisker-burn on her top lip, courtesy of Nick's stubble.

Any minute now she was going to start giggling hysterically, she thought, and bit the inside of her lip.

'So, Ronnie, the children tell me you've painted their bedrooms with spaceships and clowns and all sorts of things,' Clare said, settling in beside her as they walked up to the front door. 'That's very good of you.'

Was that a leading question? Maybe.

'It was a pleasure,' she told Clare. 'I enjoyed it. I love decorating, especially when it's interesting like that. And the children make it all worth it, they're so pleased when you've finished.'

'They certainly were pleased, they've talked about nothing else,' their grandmother confided, and Ronnie felt a flicker of alarm. Had the children inadvertently given away more than they, in fact, knew?

Holy Moses, she thought. Get out of that!

But it was easy. Conversation moved on to more general talk of the house as they all sat round the kitchen table. Clare was putting the finishing touches to Sunday lunch, to which they were all, of course, invited, and Ronnie for one was more than ready for it. Missing breakfast hadn't done anything for her, and she was feeling a little light-headed.

'Sherry, anybody?' Peter offered, and Ronnie shook her head.

'No, thank you, I won't.'

'I'm driving,' Nick said regretfully.

'Not till later.'

'Not that much later. I'd like to get back straight after lunch, if you don't mind. I've got quite a lot to do on the house still.'

'You could have a small one,' Clare coaxed. Nick shook his head. 'No, I won't. Anyway, I had quite a bit last night.'

'Oh? Celebrating the house?'

His neck coloured slightly and he avoided Ronnie's eye. 'Yes—I took Ronnie to a hotel for dinner to thank her for all her help.'

And make of that what you will, Ronnie thought with rising hysteria.

'Daddy fell over his breakfast,' Amy said, apropos of absolutely nothing, and their eyes swivelled to him. Had they linked the two?

'However did you manage that?' Clare asked in surprise.

'He put it on the floor,' Ben informed them importantly. 'He didn't realise his trousers were so splashed—that's why he's got egg all up them.'

Nick closed his eyes, and Ronnie would have laid odds he was counting. She rushed in to rescue him. 'Maybe it didn't show when it was wet,' she offered.

'It's *yellow*,' Ben said, as if he were talking to an idiot child.

'Whatever. I'm sure he won't do it again.' She shifted her attention back to Ben's grandparents. 'Have you seen the house yet?'

Peter shook his head. 'No. Nick's keeping us in suspense. He said it was so dreadful we'd have a fit if we saw it too early. I don't think he credits us with any imagination.'

Funny, Ronnie thought. I would have credited you with altogether too much. 'It's wonderful. Lots of character. It's got a lovely big entrance hall—I think that's so important, don't you?'

Nick shot her a grateful look, and the conversation ebbed and flowed as they ate their meal. Ronnie's light head settled down, and Clare and Peter stopped asking awkward questions and concentrated on the children.

'So, when are you bringing them back to us?' Clare asked as they sipped tea in the drawing room.

'Next weekend—I'm on call then—if that's all right?'

'Of course it's all right. And you'll be here for Mothering Sunday, won't you? In three weeks.'

'Yes—yes, we'll be here for that, don't worry.'

'Good.' Clare stood up. 'Come on, children, let's go and pack your things so that you can get off nice and early. You heard what Daddy said—lots to do.'

'His bedroom's a real mess, but he says he doesn't mind,' Ben told her as they went out.

'Is it?'

Nick laughed. 'Oh, yes. But it doesn't matter. It'll probably be the last thing that gets done. I need to sort out the bits people see, and the garden's clamouring for attention, too. There just aren't enough hours in the day.'

'Well, you know we're always happy to have the children so you can work late at night if you want to, but I expect you'll be moving in soon.'

'On Friday—and they have to go to school, of course, but thank you, Peter. Perhaps in the holidays—or maybe I'll get an au pair.'

Peter laughed. 'You've said that before.'

'I know. I just don't fancy having a stranger in the house.'

'You ought to get married again,' his father-in-law said calmly.

There was a second of shocked silence, then Nick let his breath out on a gust. 'Ah—I don't think so. Not yet. And, anyway, it's not a very good reason.'

'It's as good as most.'

Ronnie busied herself with her teacup and tried to be invisible. This was the *last* conversation she'd anticipated!

They were saved by Clare, coming downstairs with the children, bags in tow. 'All ready.'

Nick stood up with alacrity. 'Wonderful. Thank you so much. I'm sorry you had to take monster here to A and E.'

'Any time.' She laughed and tousled Ben's head, and he smiled up at her, clearly devoted. 'Right, let's get these bags in the car.'

They all trooped outside and without thinking, Nick opened the boot. There, as large as life and a dead giveaway, were two overnight bags.

For a moment they all froze. Then Clare looked at Nick, then at Ronnie, and smiled a gentle, understanding smile. She said nothing, just put the children's luggage in the boot, shut the lid and kissed them all goodbye. She paused by Ronnie as she opened the passenger door, and patted her shoulder.

'It's about time,' she said softly, and Ronnie felt tears fill her eyes.

She said nothing. Indeed, she couldn't have spoken if her life had depended on it. She just leaned over and gave Clare's cheek a grateful kiss, then slid into the car beside Nick. Clare closed the door and stood back, and they pulled away, the children waving through the back window.

'Whoops,' Nick muttered quietly.

Ronnie leaned back against the headrest and said nothing. She was still speechless and, anyway, she was too busy absorbing the implications of Clare's remark.

There was no opportunity for them to talk again that day—or not at length. Nick wanted to ask what Clare had said, but he had a feeling he didn't want to know—and, anyway, the children were there with their antennae going.

They went round to the new house so Ronnie could pick up her car, and while the children ran upstairs to have another look at their bedrooms, Nick put Ronnie's case into her boot to avoid another embarrassing incident.

'Do you think she realised what was going on?' he asked, in the vain hope that Ronnie would say no.

Instead she gave him a wary smile. 'Yes, she did. She said it was about time.'

He groaned and dropped his head against the roof of the car. 'Damn.'

Ronnie laid a gentle hand on his shoulder and squeezed. 'Nick, it's all right. You're a healthy adult, and it's been four years. They live in the real world. Anyway, they love you and they want you to be happy.'

'But do they want to be lied to? Because that's what I did, countless times today.'

'So ring them up and tell them, when the children are in bed. Use your mobile and go and sit in the car, so they don't hear you. Explain.'

And he would have done, if he'd felt able to. He just didn't know where to start, because the truth was he didn't know what he felt about Ronnie.

All he knew was that since he'd met her nothing had been the same, and he didn't think it ever would be again.

Ryan O'Connor went home the next day, three weeks after his stabbing, still tender but much more his old self, to the extent that Ronnie felt sure he'd overdo it.

Still, he was a doctor, an intelligent man who knew the risks better than most. She threatened him with death if he ended up back in there, but he just grinned.

'Don't fuss,' he said mildly, and carried on packing up his wash things.

'Just doing my job.'

'I know.' He lifted his head. 'So, how's it going with Nick?'

She gave a weak smile. 'His in-laws just found out about us.'

Ryan winced. 'Uh-oh. Tricky one. I remember when Ann's parents found out about me and Ginny—I thought they'd have apoplexy.'

Ronnie laughed. 'Actually, her mother was wonderful. She said it was about time.'

'Good. I agree. It's just going to be hard to make the man see it. We can be extraordinarily obtuse. Keep me posted.'

Ginny appeared then, putting an end to their conversation, and, after handing him all the necessary paperwork, Ronnie kissed his cheek and sent him home with his wife. She was sorry to see him go. He'd been an excellent patient really and, being a fellow professional, she'd been able to treat him differently.

Ah, well, she thought. There were plenty of other patients that needed her attention, and plenty who were interesting people, if you bothered to find out enough about them.

Mrs Eddison, for instance, who was back in again with her perforated bowel and stoma that refused to heal properly. She'd been a Tiller girl in her youth, and had danced at the London Palladium. Not that you'd ever know it to look at her now, with her arthritis and other problems, but if you sat and talked to her, Ronnie thought, she was fascinating.

Ronnie went to see her now, to change the dressing on her stoma and see if there was any progress in the skin which had broken down.

'Hello, dear,' Winnie said with a cheery smile. 'Did you have a nice weekend with your young man?'

Ronnie nearly dropped the dish of swabs. 'I had a lovely weekend, thank you,' she replied, refusing to be drawn. Surely she didn't know about Nick?

Apparently not. 'You must have a young man,' the woman coaxed, but Ronnie wouldn't fall for it. Not for the world would she discuss her private life with this lively and interesting perpetrator of gossip! 'That Vicky, now,' Winnie went on, 'she had a lovely weekend with David. They were planning the wedding.'

Winnie lay back with a sigh. 'I remember planning my wedding, only I was older than her, of course. I'd worked on the stage for eight years, so I must have been twenty-six when I met Bob, and twenty-eight when we got married. Just before the coronation, it was—nearly fifty years ago. He died on our ruby wedding anniversary. It was such a shame, but at least he made it. I would have been ever so cross if he'd died the day before!'

Ronnie chuckled. 'I don't suppose he'd have dared.'

'Probably not! Oh, dear, I did miss him though, at first. Still do, in a way.'

'I can imagine,' Ronnie said sympathetically. And for the first time she began to have some inkling of what her patients were going through when they described feelings of grief. Loving Nick, it made her realise just what losing him would do to her. If nothing else, then, her affair with him would make her a better nurse and a better person, because it had given her a greater understanding.

She supposed she should be grateful. Just now, she was too busy alternating between hope and despair, like a demented see-saw.

'Penny for 'em,' Winnie Eddison said.

Ronnie laughed. 'Not likely! Well, it looks as if the skin's beginning to heal again. That's good news. Now all we need is a bit of progress on the inside, and we'll have you home again!'

'Don't hurry on my account, dear,' Winnie said. 'I'm quite enjoying myself with all this company. I hated it when I went home before.'

Ronnie carefully placed the new stoma bag, sealed it firmly onto the skin and pulled off her gloves, dropping them into the midst of all the other disposable bits and pieces on the trolley and wrapping them securely. 'Have you ever thought of going into a residential home? Not a nursing home, you don't need that, but a residential home for the active elderly? You might enjoy the company.'

'I was thinking that myself,' Winnie confessed. 'I don't suppose you could help me find out about it?'

'I can get the hospital social worker to come and talk to you—she has all sorts of contacts. I'll arrange it if you like.'

'Oh, please. It'll help pass the time if nothing else, and you never know.'

Ronnie gave her hand a quick squeeze. 'I'll see what we can do,' she promised, and wheeled the trolley back to the treatment room to clear up her debris.

Vicky was in there, doing the same, and Ronnie shot her a smile. 'I gather from Mrs Eddison that you've been planning the wedding over the weekend.'

Vicky laughed. 'Sort of. It's going to be one long

set of compromises, I can tell you. He wants this, I want that, his parents want something else, and my parents say as they're paying for it they're having it another way—I thought I was going to kill them all!'

'The joys,' Ronnie said, secretly envying her colleague. She'd have given her eye-teeth to be planning her wedding to Nick. She wondered if it would ever happen, and decided it was too depressing a speculation to waste time on. She'd live for the moment, and let the future worry about itself.

Nick and the children moved into the house on Friday. Nick took the first part of the morning off to oversee the installation of the major pieces of furniture in the right rooms, and left the removal men to it for the rest of the day.

He had no choice. He had a full list, and Ronnie could tell he was like a cat on hot bricks.

'I bet I have to move almost everything round again,' he said with a resigned smile. They were in the canteen, grabbing a quick sandwich during his lunch-break, and Ronnie had managed to get away at the same time by a miracle.

'Are you going straight there after work?' she asked.

'Yes—well, I have to go and pick up the children.'

'I could do that for you,' she offered. 'I'll be finished at three today, I was on an early, so if it helps…'

He nodded gratefully. 'Brilliant,' he said round a mouthful of sandwich. 'That would be such a help. I can go straight to the house then. I'll ring you when I'm leaving here.'

So Ronnie went home and changed into jeans and a jumper and trainers—ideal for running up and down stairs with misplaced boxes, she thought! Then she waited for Nick to ring.

He finished at ten past four, and she went round to Meg's and told the children what was happening, and Ben cheered and ran for the door. Amy, though, walked with Ronnie, looking thoughtful, and she had a feeling something was wrong.

'What's the matter, sweetheart?' she asked, bending down to her.

'I don't want to leave you,' Amy confessed, and threw her arms round Ronnie's neck and burst into tears.

Oh, dear. Ronnie hugged her and rocked her, and told her that, of course, she'd still see her, just because they were moving didn't mean they wouldn't still be friends, and she'd come round and see them often, and, anyway, they'd still be coming to Meg every day so she'd see them then.

The crying hiccuped to a halt, and Amy lifted her tear-stained face from Ronnie's shoulder and sniffed. 'Promise,' she said wetly, and Ronnie promised.

'Now, let's go to the new house or Daddy will wonder what I've done with you.'

Ben was leaning on the car, watching this exchange, and he looked up at Ronnie worriedly. 'Is she all right?'

'She doesn't want to move.'

'I do!' Ben said firmly. 'It's a cool house, and I've got a spaceship bedroom, and a big garden—Dad says I can have goalposts in the garden to play football.'

Ronnie could already hear the tinkling glass from the broken windows, but she held her tongue. Maybe he'd kick it sideways across the garden.

'Right, into the car—let's go.'

Nick was already there when they arrived, organising the movement of a couple of large pieces of furniture, and Ronnie made herself useful with the teapot while the children ran excitedly through the house, re-acquainting themselves with all their furniture. Then at last the door closed behind the removal men and Nick turned to her with a sigh.

'Well, that's it. Everything's here, except for our clothes and bits and pieces at the other house.'

Ronnie swallowed the lump in her throat. She didn't want them to go any more than Amy did, and she was dreading the silence from next door once they'd gone. She'd got so used to hearing their voices over the past month or two.

'Come and see,' he said, and she followed him round, looking at all the furniture, the boxes, the huge amount he still had to do.

'We need curtains, of course. I don't suppose you know anybody?'

'Meg will,' she told him with a smile.

'Bless her, she's the fount of all knowledge. Well, the children go to their grandparents for the weekend, and hopefully by Sunday night I will have got the place a bit straighter and the other house cleared, even if we haven't got curtains. I'm sure I can find something to put up.'

'Do you want a hand?' Ronnie offered.

'If you've got time. I seem to be taking up all your time recently.'

She didn't know how to answer that, so she ignored it and went with the first part of his answer. 'I've got time,' she told him. In truth she had nothing else. She couldn't remember how she'd spent her time before they'd all come along. Perhaps she'd better start thinking about it!

It was an exhausting weekend. Nick was on call, and several times he left Ronnie unpacking books or crockery or such-like while he went back to the hospital.

It was strange, handling all his things. She wondered how many of them Anna had chosen, and how Anna would have felt about her. At least her parents didn't seem to object too violently. She put a handful of books on the shelf in the snug and sat back on her heels.

She'd hoped things might have moved on a little since last weekend, or that they would have talked more about Anna's parents and their reaction, but Nick had been remarkably distant in a way.

No, not distant. He'd just avoided any chances for intimacy of any sort. There had been no kisses, no hugs—not even this weekend, while they'd been alone.

She heard him come back, and quickly scrubbed away the tears she hadn't realised were on her cheeks. 'Hi—I'm in here.'

He came in and stood behind her. 'Wonderful. Thank you. It's beginning to look like a home.'

She stood up, brushing her hands on her jeans, and gave him a slightly off-key smile. 'Do you mind if I go home?' she said. 'I've got lots to do, and I've got a bit of a headache.'

'No, of course not. Thank you so much for all your help. You've been wonderful.'

He drew her into his arms and hugged her, then pressed a kiss to her brow. 'Go on, you go home. I'll be all right now. Thank you, Ronnie.'

'You're welcome,' she said huskily and, grabbing her keys from by the door, she let herself out. She managed to get home before the tears fell, but only just. Meg found her slumped over the wheel of her car on the drive, sobbing as if her heart would break. She took her friend inside and made her a cup of tea and gave her lots of sage advice while Ronnie sniffed and blew her nose and howled again.

Finally, though, Meg had to go and collect Jimmy from his father, and there was nothing to distract Ronnie from the knowledge that nothing had changed. Nick still didn't want to acknowledge her as part of his life, and Ronnie could do nothing about it.

CHAPTER TEN

WINNIE EDDISON went home at the end of the next week. She'd found a residential home that could take her from the beginning of April, and as she had her own funding, she was able to move at her own convenience, instead of waiting for the wheels of bureaucracy to turn.

Her daughter had taken her to look round a couple of times, and she'd come back from the second visit, bubbling over with excitement.

'You'll never guess—there's someone there I haven't seen for thirty years, but we still recognised each other. She used to be my neighbour, but then she moved away and we lost touch. Isn't that amazing?'

'And have they definitely got a space?' Ronnie asked, delighted to see her enthusiasm.

'Yes—I'm going next Friday. Well, if I'm all right by then. I have to have a few days at home to pack everything up and sort my things out.'

'We'll ask Mr Sarazin when he comes down,' she said. 'He'll let you go as soon as you're ready, don't worry. Have you got someone to move you?'

'My daughter—she'll help. I can have all my things. There's a big empty room, and I can take all of my personal bits and pieces with me—letters from Bob when we were courting, things of the children's—you know the sort of thing.'

Ronnie did. She had a drawer in her bedroom that was filling up with things—a note from Nick, a drawing from Amy, Ben's version of his bedroom, a thank-you note from him for painting all the spaceships—all sorts of little things to get out and cry over in a weak moment.

She knew just what Winnie was on about.

'Just don't make yourself overtired, packing everything up,' she cautioned.

Winnie laughed. 'Oh, no, dear. I shall sit in my chair and tell my daughter and my grandchildren what to do!'

Ronnie didn't doubt it for a minute!

She spoke to Nick about Winnie's plans when she next saw him, and he made time to go and have a look at her and chat to her about her stoma care and the care of her bowel.

'I don't see why you shouldn't go, so long as you're careful not to overdo it,' he said.

Winnie patted his hand. 'Don't you worry, I'll be all right. It's the first time since I lost Bob that I've had anything to look forward to. I feel years younger.'

Ronnie was sorry to see her go on Friday, but glad for her that everything seemed to be turning out so well. She wished she had something to look forward to in her own life, because Nick was still keeping her at arm's length, and the house next door was unbearably quiet.

She went away for the weekend rather than flagellate herself with Nick's absence, and visited her father and stepmother in Southampton. They went to Lymington and walked along the river by the yacht club, and she assiduously avoided any personal conversation.

Until, that was, her stepmother cornered her in the kitchen after Sunday lunch. 'What's wrong, Ronnie?' she asked with typical directness. 'You've dried that plate so thoroughly you've nearly rubbed the design off it.'

Ronnie put the plate down and picked up another. 'I'm in love,' she confessed. 'He's a widower, with two small children, and he won't let me in because he doesn't want to upset them.'

Kathy sighed and rested her hands in the washing-up water. 'Been there, done that,' she said softly. 'It hurts, doesn't it?'

Ronnie looked at her in puzzlement. 'I don't understand. You were widowed when Dad met you. You got married straight away—and Martin didn't have any children.'

'Martin didn't, no, but your father did. And I wasn't a widow when I met him, I was a young woman in my late twenties, and I fell hopelessly in love, but he wouldn't do anything about it because of you and Bryony. We kept our love a secret for four years, and then I met Martin, and he offered me a chance at a real relationship, so I took it.'

'And then his heart gave out.'

'Yes. He always said I broke it, because he knew I truly belonged to your father in my heart of hearts, although I did everything I could to be a good and loyal wife to him.'

'And then he died, and by then Bryony and I had grown up, so it was all right,' Ronnie said slowly. 'But that's so silly! I would have loved to have had you as a mother then! I really needed a mother so much.'

Kathy smiled. 'I tried to tell your father, but men can be very slow about these things.'

Funny, Ryan had said something very similar, Ronnie recalled. 'Oh, Kathy, I'm sorry. All those wasted years!'

'No, not wasted,' she said gently. 'I loved Martin in my own way, and he loved me. It was just different, not wasted. And your father and I are together now.

You might just have to wait a long time for your man to come to his senses. How old are the children?'

'Six and eight,' Ronnie said bleakly. 'Twelve years till they go to university.'

'By which time you'll be forty. You have to make a decision, Ronnie. Hang around and wait, or go out and make a life for yourself without him.'

'I'll never forget him.'

'Of course not. I never forgot your father, but I had a life, a very full and satisfactory one. You just have to choose.'

It gave Ronnie a great deal to think about, and later in the week she found even more to think about.

She was cleaning out her bathroom cupboards to kill the empty hours when she found her tampons. She looked at them thoughtfully. When *had* she last had a period?

Weeks ago—before the ball. Before they'd made love. Eight weeks ago, to be exact.

She sat down with a bump. Oh, God, she thought, surely not? She stared at her watch. Seven-fifteen. The supermarkets were still open. She ran down to her car, flew round to the supermarket, grabbed a pregnancy test kit off the shelf and rushed home.

Then she closeted herself in the bathroom with the test and stared at it for ages. She read the instructions about six times, then decided there was nothing else for it. She had to do the test.

She couldn't open her eyes. She daren't look at the strip. She washed her hands, flushed the loo and sat down on the lid, still with her eyes shut. She didn't want to know.

It might be negative.

She felt sick, either with anticipation or apprehension, or even just because she was pregnant.

'You don't know that,' she told herself. 'You have to look.'

It was positive. She closed her eyes, opened them again and checked, and then shut them.

'Oh, my God,' she said softly. 'I'm having a baby.'

And then she started to cry.

'Jimmy's got football—I don't suppose you could bear to have Ben and Amy, could you?' Meg asked. 'He wants me to go and watch—it's an important match, or something, and Nick's just phoned to say he's been held up at the hospital with an emergency and won't be back for ages.'

Ronnie dredged up a smile. 'No, that's fine,' she said, ignoring the fact that it was going to tear her apart. 'Of course I don't mind.'

'Brilliant. I'll send them round. They're doing their homework, and they've had something to eat, so it shouldn't be too arduous.'

Looking after Ben and Amy was never arduous to Ronnie, but she didn't bother to say so. She just threw together a packet of chocolate brownie mix and put it in the oven just as Ben and Amy pounded on the door.

'Hi, kids,' she said, welcoming them into the hall. 'Put your coats on the banisters and come and finish your homework, and then we can watch the telly.'

'Are those brownies in the oven?' Amy asked, her radar zooming in on them.

'Yes,' Ronnie said with a chuckle. 'Later. Homework first.'

They settled down at the kitchen table with a little grumble, and pulled out folded pieces of card and colouring pens.

'We have to do Mother's Day cards,' Ben said, screwing up his nose. 'We do them for Grannie.'

Oh, God, Ronnie thought, aching for them. How awful.

'I can't remember Mummy,' Amy said, sticking her tongue out of the corner of her mouth in concentration. 'I wish I had a mummy.'

'Jimmy's got two mummies,' Ben said. 'Meg, and his dad's married again, but she's bossy, he says.'

'I've got a stepmother,' Ronnie told them, sitting down at the table. 'Her name's Kathy. She's very nice.'

'I bet she was bossy when you were little.'

'She wasn't there when I was little,' Ronnie told them, wishing she had been. 'My mother died when I was eleven, but my father didn't get married again until I was twenty-two.'

'So do you 'member her? Your real mum, I mean,' Amy asked.

'Oh, yes. Sort of. I can remember quite a lot.'

'That must be nice,' Ben said. 'I don't remember much. I can remember her smell. She smelled of hospitals.'

Poor little things. Ronnie blinked. 'I'll just check the brownies,' she said, even though she knew they were nothing like ready. Anything to get away from the clear, all-seeing eyes of those children while she pulled herself together.

She could hear Amy scribbling away with her felt pens, colouring in flowers and leaves with big, wild strokes that went over the edges. Ben was being much more careful, drawing a very intricate picture of a spaceship.

'Grannie doesn't like spaceships,' Amy told him, and Ronnie intervened quickly before there was a fight.

She wondered how long it would be before her own child was sitting at the kitchen table, drawing a

Mother's Day card for her, and her hand slid down to cradle the slight bulge.

It wasn't really a bulge yet, more of a fullness, but it wouldn't be long and then she'd have to make some difficult decisions.

She'd already decided she had to tell Nick, but what happened after that, she couldn't even begin to guess at. What she didn't want was for him to marry her out of misplaced duty, and for her to spend the rest of her life trying to live up to Anna's memory.

The brownies were finally cooked, and the cards completed, and they went through to the sitting room and snacked in front of the television.

It was eight o'clock before Nick turned up, and the children were drooping and ready for bed.

'I'd invite you in for coffee, but they've had it,' Ronnie told him regretfully.

He smiled at her over their heads, a strained smile which made her think he'd probably have said no anyway, and ushered them out to the car. The silence was deafening.

Mothering Sunday dawned bright and sunny, fluffy clouds scudding across the sky, and the daffodils were nodding their heads in the stiff April breeze.

Nick was dreading the service. He'd started coming with Anna before they were married, and it had become a tradition. They'd continued to come with their own children, and since Anna's death, he'd brought Ben and Amy to put flowers on Anna's grave. It seemed appropriate, and it was a comfort to Clare because she only had her grandchildren now, and they filled the gap Anna had left.

His own mother was in Somerset, miles away and surrounded by family, so his absence didn't really hurt them and besides, he found himself locked into the ritual.

It didn't hurt any more like it had at first, but for some reason this year it seemed strange, as if they should have moved on.

He wondered if the children felt it, or if it was just him. He'd taken his ring off this week and put it away. After four years he felt it was time, and he realised he'd been hiding behind it. He was all stirred up because of Ronnie, of course. He'd been avoiding her, but it didn't make any difference. He still thought about her every minute that he wasn't with her, and the nights were getting harder and harder to deal with.

He'd thought moving to the new house would help, because he wouldn't have to listen to her through the wall, humming softly as she went about her chores, the rapid patter of her feet on the stairs, the roar of her vacuum cleaner, the clash of her dustbin lid in the garden outside.

Now he had nothing but an eerie silence after the children were asleep, broken only by the occasional car going past, and the sound of cats fighting on the fence at the bottom of the garden.

Nothing, in fact, to distract him from missing her.

He threw open the window and drew in a lungful of fresh country air. If only he could be sure their relationship would work, but he was sure Ronnie wouldn't want to take on his children. She would want a family of her own, not a man with a past and children with scars that went so deep he thought they'd never heal.

Amy had started wetting the bed again, and Ben was grumpy and difficult, despite the spaceships. They talked about Ronnie constantly, and clearly missed her as much as he did.

And he didn't know what to do about it.

He went to wake them, to take their cards in to their grandmother. Peter had just left to prepare the church for communion, and if they left it any later Clare would be busy.

He went into the room next door which had been Anna's room, and woke them.

'Rise and shine, kids. You've got to give Grannie her cards.'

Ben sat up, scrubbing his eyes and blinking, and Amy started to cry.

'I wet the bed,' she sobbed, and with a quiet sigh Nick took her in his arms and cuddled her.

'It's all right, darling. Don't worry. We'll wash the sheets for Grannie and give you a bath. Let's change your nightie and you can go and give her your card.'

'I don't want to,' she sobbed. 'I want to give it to Ronnie.'

Oh, Lord, he thought. Not this again. Her teacher had come out on Friday afternoon when he'd picked them up from school, and had smiled at him curiously. 'I gather congratulations are in order,' she said.

His jaw had dropped. 'Excuse me?'

'Oh—have I misunderstood? Amy told me she was making two Mother's Day cards—one for her grandmother, and one for her new mother.'

He'd quickly disabused her of that notion, but Amy had been harder to persuade, and it seemed he'd still failed to get through.

'Darling, I explained this to you on Friday,' he said patiently. 'Ronnie's not your mother. She's just a friend. She's a very special friend, but that doesn't mean she's your mother.'

'But I want a mummy!' Amy sobbed. 'I want Ronnie!'

'So do I,' Ben said quietly from his bed. 'She's not

bossy. Jimmy doesn't really like his stepmother, but Ronnie's cool. She doesn't tell me what to do, and she's funny.'

Nick swallowed. 'But... I don't know how Ronnie would feel about it.'

'Why don't you ask her?' Clare said from behind him, and he looked over his shoulder and stared dumbly at her.

'Ask her?' he croaked.

'Mmm. Now.'

'Now?'

'Yes. Ring her and invite her for lunch, and ask her. Or go now.'

He looked at his watch. He couldn't go now, because he'd miss the service and, dread it or not, he had to be there to help the children through it. They always took flowers up to the altar with all the other children, and had them blessed by Peter, and then went out into the churchyard to put them on Anna's grave.

He had to be there for that.

'I'll ring her,' he said, and stood up. 'Um, Amy's wet the bed, by the way.'

'Oh, sweetheart, never mind. Let's give you a nice bath, shall we?'

He left the children in Clare's capable hands and ran downstairs to the study. It was quiet in there, and he could speak to Ronnie without interruptions.

He dialled her number, frantically trying to remember if she was on duty or not, and then nearly dropped the phone when she answered.

'Ronnie?' he said, and his voice cracked with emotion.

'Nick? What's wrong?' she said, instantly picking up on it.

'Nothing. Ronnie, can you come for lunch?'

There was a second of silence, then she said in a puzzled voice, 'I thought you were at Anna's parents'?'

'We are. Can you find it? I can give you directions.'

Did he sound desperate? It would be strange if he didn't, he thought, because suddenly it seemed as if his whole future depended on her answer.

'I can find it,' she said after a moment. 'Just remind me.'

He gave her quick directions, and then said goodbye. All he could do now was wait.

'Well?' Clare said when he went back upstairs.

'She's coming.'

The children shrieked with delight, and Clare smiled her encouragement.

'It'll be all right, Nick. You'll see.'

He hoped so. He really, really hoped so...

Nick had sounded odd. Strained, as if things were not quite right. Ronnie didn't know what was wrong, she couldn't even hazard a guess, but she knew he needed her, and that was enough.

She had a quick bath and put on a smart day dress and a cardigan. It was too warm for a coat, she thought, and looked at her watch. If she left now she would be hopelessly early, but she couldn't bear to hang around.

It only took just less than an hour to get there, and she arrived at eleven. She could hear singing in the church, and there was no sign of them. She didn't know what to do, but the chances were that Nick was in the church. Perhaps she should go in and find him?

Or just slip in and sit at the back.

Or wait in the car.

Which?

She went into the church, lit with the brilliant sunshine of the early April day, and Clare turned her head and beckoned to her.

She went, tiptoeing down the aisle at the side and slipping into the pew between Clare and Nick. He took her hand and squeezed it, and didn't let go.

That was fine. She didn't either. She sneaked a glance at him out of the corner of her eye, and saw the strain etched on his face. Whatever did he want? What on earth could be wrong?

She forced herself to concentrate on the service, and listened to the children who were gathered at the altar as they sang 'All Things Bright and Beautiful'.

It brought a huge lump to her throat, and Clare pressed a tissue into her hand.

'Thanks,' she whispered, and blotted her eyes. How silly. It had just been such a long time since her mother had died, and this service brought it all slamming back. Besides which, she was very emotional at the moment anyway.

She laid her hand with the crumpled tissue in it over her baby and hung on, watching as the children in turn took their little posies up to Peter for blessing. Nick stood up as the children turned, and she remembered that Ben and Amy were going to put their flowers on their mother's grave.

Oh, Lord.

Ronnie blinked again, and as she opened her eyes Amy saw her.

'Ronnie!' she cried excitedly, and ran and threw herself into Ronnie's arms, almost squashing her daffodils.

'Hello, darling,' Ronnie said unsteadily. She gave her a kiss, then looked up at Nick for help.

'Come on, sweetheart. Let's do the flowers. You can see Ronnie in a minute.'

He held out his hand, and after a moment Amy went,

skipping down the aisle. Ben grinned at Ronnie, and she smiled back and wondered how long it would be before she could creep away and have a good howl.

Clare's hand settled discreetly on her knee and gave it a comforting squeeze, and she blinked and smiled back and tried not to lose it completely.

Then the children came back inside, and Amy slipped into the seat beside her and pressed a daffodil into her hand. 'I saved one for you,' Amy said, and the tears refused to be held back any longer.

'Thank you,' Ronnie whispered and, closing her eyes, she let the tears slide unheeded down her cheeks. Her arm wrapped itself round Amy's shoulders, and Amy climbed onto her lap, almost crushing the daffodil as she snuggled into Ronnie's arms.

Ben wriggled up beside her, and she put her arm around him and hugged him too. 'Hi, spaceman,' she said softly, and he grinned.

She met Nick's eyes over his head, and the longing in them made her heart race.

What did he want? What could it be?

Then, finally, the service was over and, taking her hand in his, Nick led her out into the churchyard and round the corner. There was a grave there under a tree, beautifully tended, the headstone a very simple memorial to a young woman who should never have died as she had, with so much to live for.

'Anna, this is Ronnie,' Nick said quietly. 'I love her, and the children love her, and I hope she loves me, because I want her to marry me and help me bring up our children. I know you would have liked her, and she would have liked you, even though you're very different. I'll always love you, and treasure your memory, but I need to move on and so do the children. I just wanted you to meet her.'

Ronnie couldn't believe what he was saying. All you have to do is wait, Ryan had said, in one of their many conversations, but she hadn't dared believe him.

And now, today of all days, or perhaps because it was Mothering Sunday, Nick was asking her to marry him.

He turned to her, his eyes full of hope and fear and uncertainty, and looked down into her eyes.

'Veronica, will you marry me?' he asked softly.

'Oh, yes,' she said, tears welling helplessly. 'Of course I will. I love you—I love you all, so much.'

She reached out her arms and gathered the children to her side, and Nick's arms came round them all.

And then the shadow of the clouds was chased away by the sun, and the children's flowers on their mother's grave were bathed with gold...

'So, when's the great day going to be, and where?' Peter asked as they all sat round the table for lunch. 'Will you get married in Suffolk, or do you have a family home?'

'My father and stepmother live in Southampton,' she told them, 'but it isn't really home. I suppose where I live now is home, but I don't have a parish, really. I sometimes go to services in the hospital chapel, but not often. I haven't really thought about it.'

'You could get married here,' Amy said brightly. 'Grandad does weddings.'

Ronnie looked up, startled by the suggestion, and met Clare's eyes. 'You could. It's up to you, but it would be lovely if you were married here.'

'Wouldn't you mind?' she asked, thinking again of Anna.

'No, and nor would Anna. Nick's in our family now,

and we'd like you to be as well—if you don't mind, that is. Maybe you'd rather not.'

Ronnie swallowed. 'What about Nick?' she asked, turning to him. He smiled tenderly. 'Whatever you want. I just want to marry you. I'll do whatever you like.'

'In which case,' she said unsteadily, 'I can't think of anywhere I'd rather we were married than here.'

'Good, then that's settled,' Peter said, settling back with a smile.

'Um… Do you do christenings as well?' she asked, and Nick nearly choked.

'Ronnie?' he mouthed silently.

She smiled serenely. 'Yes,' she said, and watched the shock turn to joy in his eyes.

'Are we going to have a baby?' Amy asked, looking curiously from one to the other.

'Not yet,' Ronnie told them. 'We'll get married first.'

'I'd better look at my diary,' Peter said, and beamed at them. 'I wonder if I've got a space next week.'

EPILOGUE

SHE was so beautiful. Tiny features, perfectly formed, her fingers curled over his as she slept—Nick thought she was wonderful.

About as wonderful as Ben and Amy, and nearly as beautiful as her mother.

He looked across at Ronnie, slender again after the long months of pregnancy, and caught her eye. She smiled, a contented, loving smile, and hugged the children. They stood next to her, one each side, as devoted as ever and much more settled now, and he wondered how he could ever have thought Ronnie might be bad for them.

Not Ronnie, exactly, but a relationship with her. In fact, the last year had been one of the happiest of his life, and it seemed fitting that they should be gathered here—in the church where he and Anna had started their marriage, where their children had been christened, where Anna had been laid to rest, and where he and Ronnie had been married just ten months ago—for the christening of their daughter Elisabeth Anna.

She was Elisabeth for Ronnie's mother, and it had been Ronnie's idea to give her Anna as a second name.

He had been deeply moved by her gesture, more so by the fact that it wasn't just an empty gesture, it was an acknowledgement of the fact that Anna would never be forgotten, that her name wouldn't be avoided, and that her children would grow up able to talk about her freely with both parents.

Clare and Peter had been wonderful, too. They had

welcomed Ronnie into the family with open arms, and had made her totally at home. It was down to Ronnie's easy friendliness and generous nature that it had all worked so well, Nick thought, and that, instead of Clare and Peter losing him and the children, they'd gained another daughter and another grandchild.

Because the children now had three sets of grandparents, and all of them were assembled there in the church to see little Beth christened.

She started to squirm, the service failing to hold her attention, and she chewed her fist fretfully.

'She's hungry,' Nick said softly to Ronnie, and she took the baby from him, cradling the little one against her shoulder and rocking her gently.

The sun slanting through the window touched them all with gold, and as Peter drew the service to a close, Nick met Ronnie's eyes again and smiled.

'I love you,' he mouthed, and her smile softened, a light in her eyes only for him.

'I love you, too,' she replied silently.

And Beth, not to be left out, burped milk all over Ronnie's shoulder.

'Whoops,' Amy said, giggling deliciously. 'Beth's christened you now!'

Nick took his youngest daughter back while Ronnie wiped her shoulder, and she snuggled against him with a contented sigh. Wind, then, not hunger.

The service having ended, they drifted out into the churchyard and headed back towards the house. As they went, Nick glanced back over his shoulder at Anna's grave. It was bathed in sunlight, the flowers the children had put there that morning nodding in the breeze, and he felt peace steal over him.

He'd never thought he'd be happy again. Not truly

happy, like this, with a wonderful wife and another precious child, a fresh start for all of them, hope for the future.

Life truly was good…

FREE
4 BOOKS
AND A SURPRISE GIFT!

We would like to take this opportunity to thank you for reading this Mills & Boon® book by offering you the chance to take FOUR more specially selected titles from the Medical Romance™ series absolutely FREE! We're also making this offer to introduce you to the benefits of the Reader Service™—

- ★ FREE home delivery
- ★ FREE monthly Newsletter
- ★ FREE gifts and competitions
- ★ Exclusive Reader Service discounts
- ★ Books available before they're in the shops

Accepting these FREE books and gift places you under no obligation to buy; you may cancel at any time, even after receiving your free shipment. Simply complete your details below and return the entire page to the address below. *You don't even need a stamp!*

YES! Please send me 4 free Medical Romance books and a surprise gift. I understand that unless you hear from me, I will receive 6 superb new titles every month for just £2.40 each, postage and packing free. I am under no obligation to purchase any books and may cancel my subscription at any time. The free books and gift will be mine to keep in any case.

MOEC

Ms/Mrs/Miss/Mr ....Initials ....
BLOCK CAPITALS PLEASE

Surname ....

Address ....

....

....Postcode ....

Send this whole page to:
UK: FREEPOST CN81, Croydon, CR9 3WZ
EIRE: PO Box 4546, Kilcock, County Kildare (stamp required)